CW01498675

STAY HAPPY

A Story Inspired by Jack Forrest-Rickard

Written through the life of Felix Asher

Dedication

FOR MY MUM, DENISE

You taught me the strength of quiet resilience and the depth of unconditional love. Even when life didn't give you the softest edges, you softened them for me. Your courage lives in every page of this book.

FOR MY HUSBAND, ASH

For loving me through every version of myself, the broken, the brave, and the becoming. You stood beside me when the storms came, and you stayed. This story wouldn't be whole without you in it.

FOR MY FRIEND, AMY

My Cherry. My lighthouse. For seeing the real me when I was still figuring him out. You brought laughter to the darkest days and reminded me that chosen family can save lives.

FOR EVERY SINGLE SUPPORTER OF JFR.PRODUCTIONS

You've turned whispers into waves. You listened when I shared, you showed up when it mattered, and you proved that storytelling, honest, raw, and unfiltered, can change everything. This is your story too.

And finally... FOR ME

Because I survived. Because I found the words. Because I chose to stay. And because I finally understand that healing isn't about forgetting what happened, it's about becoming who you were always meant to be in spite of it.

PROLOGUE

STAY HAPPY

People always thought Felix was the happy one.Even when life cracked at the edges, he was the one smiling. The one saying, *"It's fine."* The one who cracked the jokes, posted the videos, lit up the room, even when he was crumbling in the dark.

"STAY HAPPY."

That was his catchphrase. His armour. His lifeline. He said it so often, people started saying it back. But what most didn't know was that it wasn't just a feel-good phrase. It was a survival tactic.

Felix Asher had been many things in his thirty-three years. A dreamer. A people-pleaser. A boy searching for safety in all the wrong places. A man betrayed not once, but twice, each time by someone who swore they never would. A survivor of trauma. A lover of light. A fighter for peace. He had battled grief, silence, weight, shame, and the kind of loneliness that can't be seen in photos. And yet somehow, he found a way to keep going.

Not just going. Growing.

This is not the story of a man who had it easy. It's the story of a man who had every reason to give up, and chose, again and again, not to.

Because happiness wasn't handed to Felix. He built it. From rubble. From pain. From truth.

This is his story.

And if it feels like yours too… maybe that's no coincidence.

CHAPTER ONE

A Little Light in a Chaotic World

Felix Asher came into the world quietly, not in silence, but in something close to it.

He was born into a house that held its breath. The kind of place where emotions lingered in corners but were rarely spoken out loud. His mum did her best. She worked hard, smiled when she could, and loved him in her own way, but Felix could always sense that life had worn her down long before he arrived. She was strong, but not always present. Tired, but still trying. And her silence became one of Felix's first lullabies.

There was no father in the picture. No deep voice down the hallway, no protective arms, no one to throw a ball with or threaten the boys who made fun of him. He never really asked where that man had gone, maybe because no one ever offered answers, and maybe because deep down, even as a child, he knew the space that man left behind was never meant to be filled by him in the first place.

Instead, Felix looked for protection in other places, teachers, neighbours, the fathers of friends, anyone older, anyone male, anyone who might *see* him and stay. But they never did. Some got too close too fast, others vanished without warning. The cycle repeated so often, it started to feel like a pattern he was somehow responsible for. Like something about him wasn't quite enough to hold their interest.

Still, he smiled. He adapted.

From a young age, Felix became an expert in scanning rooms for mood shifts. He could feel tension before it entered a space. He knew when to make himself small and when to turn himself up like a volume knob, cracking jokes, dancing around, becoming the entertainment when the energy needed lifting. He was a child, but already, he understood what it meant to shape-shift to survive.

And then, at seven years old, everything changed.

She arrived on the TV like a beam of glittering electricity. Amber.

Felix remembered the moment vividly, her blonde ponytail swaying, her eyes locked onto the camera like she knew a secret, her voice full of rhythm and confidence and something fierce. She wore sparkle like it was battle armour, and when she moved, it wasn't just choreography, it was liberation.

Felix was *spellbound*.

He sat cross-legged in front of the screen, mouth slightly open, eyes wide. And in that moment, something inside him, something quiet and aching, felt seen. Not by his mum. Not by the world. But by her. By Amber.

She became more than a popstar to him. She was proof. Proof that being loud, expressive, creative, emotional, all the things he was constantly told to tone down, could be powerful. Beautiful, even. She was freedom with a mic. And Felix, in his own way, made a silent vow that night: *one day, I'll be like her*.

He taped her music videos on old VHS tapes, mimicked her moves in his bedroom, and built performances in his head like sacred rituals. His sister would laugh sometimes, calling him dramatic, and his mum would smile, unsure of what to make of his obsession. But no one stopped him. And that was enough.

Amber became the lighthouse in his storm. A symbol of who he might be one day, if he could just make it through the chaos around him.

At school, life was harder. He was too soft for the boys and too loud for the teachers. They called him "sensitive" like it was a flaw. He'd hear whispers in the changing rooms at P.E, feel the sting of side glances, and brush off jokes that landed like punches. But inside, he carried Amber's energy like armour. When he felt weak, he imagined her on stage, powerful, unbothered, unforgettable, and reminded himself that one day, he'd get to dance through his own pain, too.

There were good moments, ones that shimmered like gold threads through the grey. Summer nights when the house was warm with laughter, holidays when things felt light for a while, small pockets of joy that came with family rituals and silly home videos. He clung to those, replaying them in his mind like songs he didn't want to forget.

But deep down, Felix was always searching.

Searching for safety. For acceptance. For someone to wrap around him like a promise and not let go.

And that hunger, that craving to be *loved right*, it stayed with him, shaping the way he moved through the world. He loved too deeply, gave too quickly, and forgave far too often. But how could he not? When all he ever wanted was to be chosen, and kept.

He didn't know it yet, but that desire would one day cost him more than he thought he could survive.

CHAPTER TWO

The Boy Who Loved Too Deeply

Felix Asher had a heart that didn't just beat, it ached. From the earliest age, he carried a tenderness that didn't belong in a world so sharp.

It was never enough for Felix to just be liked, he needed to be held. Not always physically, but emotionally. He craved connection the way other kids craved sweets. If someone looked at him like he mattered, he was already halfway in love with them. A smile, a kind word, a seat saved at lunch, it didn't take much. Just enough to make him feel chosen.

Because underneath the laughter, the big eyes, and the daydreams, there lived a quiet truth:
Felix never really felt like anyone's first choice.

He learned early on how to shrink himself to fit other people's needs. If someone was sad, he'd be funny. If they were angry, he'd be still. If they were distant, he'd get louder, not out of arrogance, but desperation. He wanted to be seen. Wanted to be kept. Wanted to be someone's safe place so that maybe, just maybe, they'd become his.

At school, he was the kid who clung to teachers like lifeboats. He'd stay behind after class to help pack up, just for a little extra attention. He thrived on praise, lived for those rare moments when someone older smiled at him like he was more than background noise.

It wasn't about being dramatic. It was about being hungry. Starved, even. Not for food, but for a kind of love that didn't walk away.

At home, his world was quiet, but never cold.

His mum, Begonia, was his lighthouse. She wasn't perfect. She worked long hours and sometimes her eyes were heavy with things she didn't say. But Felix never doubted her love. Not once.

She made sure he had everything he needed, but more importantly, she made sure he felt loved. She'd tuck him in at night and kiss the top of his head, whispering, "You've got a heart made of gold, Felix. Don't let this world dim it."

And he never forgot those words.

She'd sit and watch his little performances in the living room, clapping even when he forgot the moves. She saved his drawings, told him he was brave when he cried, and once, when a boy at school made fun of the way he talked, she said, "Don't change a single thing about yourself. Not for anyone."

Her love was soft, constant, and safe, the kind that wrapped around you and stayed, even when everything else felt uncertain.

Still, there were spaces Felix needed filled that even she couldn't reach.
And that's where the world got messy.

There was one teacher, Mr. Harland, who once told Felix during a reading group, "You've got something special, you know." Felix carried those seven words around like a secret talisman, repeating them in his head for weeks, clinging to them on days when the world felt too cold.

That same winter, he met Clarke.

Clarke was a boy in his class with freckled cheeks and a mischievous laugh. They bonded over music, specifically Oasis, a band Felix pretended to enjoy just to stay close to him. He would study the way Clarke tied his shoelaces, the way he flicked his fringe to one side, the way his trainers lit up when he ran.

They became inseparable, or so Felix believed. They'd walk home together some days, talk about the latest crush Clarke had, and once, when it rained too hard, they hid under a tree and made up a handshake that Felix practised alone for weeks.

One night, Felix wrote Clarke's name on a scrap of paper and drew a small heart next to it, hiding it in his art folder. He wasn't sure what it meant, he just knew it made him feel warm.

But by the time spring arrived, something shifted. Clarke started sitting with the louder boys. He laughed when they mimicked Felix's voice. When Felix tried to sit beside him at lunch one day, Clarke slid down the bench and said, "There's no space," even though there was plenty.

Felix never mentioned it. He just nodded and walked away.

That night, he tore up the note.

That was the first time Felix felt the sting of almost being loved. It wouldn't be the last.

He kept loving anyway.

Every new friend was a fresh chance to prove he was worthy of loyalty. He'd lend pencils, give out snacks, offer his turn at games. He didn't think of it as buying affection, he genuinely wanted to be kind. But part of him hoped that if he just gave enough, someone might finally stay.

He once asked his mum, when he was about ten, "Why do I always feel too much?"

Begonia paused, looked him in the eyes, and said, "Because you're alive in a way most people never dare to be. And that's a gift, not a weakness."

He remembered that. Even when people broke him.

He never met his dad. Never even saw a picture. When he asked about him once, Begonia simply said, "He wasn't ready to be a parent," and pulled him into a hug that lasted longer than usual.

That was the end of it. No drama. Just a door that stayed closed. But her embrace softened the edges of that silence.

Still, that absence became a blueprint, the first of many men who would leave quietly, without explanation.

So Felix looked elsewhere.

He started gravitating toward older boys, ones who could offer a sense of safety, admiration, or even just presence. Teammates. Mentors. Friends' older brothers. Anyone who looked strong, confident, settled. He didn't want anything from them, just to be seen by them.

Just to matter.

That need would eventually lead him somewhere dark. But not yet. For now, he was still the boy with the open heart and too many empty spaces.

CHAPTER THREE

When the Silence Started Speaking

Some stories don't start with thunder. Some start with a whisper that never leaves.

Felix had always thought that the world would warn you before it turned dark.

That there would be thunder. Shouting. Maybe a door slammed so hard it shook the walls. Something to mark the moment life splits in two, before and after. But it didn't happen that way for him.

The day it happened looked like any other. Grey-blue sky. Crisp air. The faint hum of a distant lawnmower. It was a Saturday, and Felix had rehearsed his lines in the mirror at least fifty times before leaving the house. His voice was a little hoarse, his backpack full of snacks and costume bits, and his stomach fluttering with something that felt like hope.

He had finally joined a local stage group.

He hadn't told many people at school, just said he had "stuff on Saturdays." Performing wasn't something the other boys talked about unless they were making fun of it. But for Felix, the stage wasn't about being seen, it was about being safe. A place where feelings weren't weaknesses, they were the point.

Begonia had packed his bag the night before, folding his hoodie with the kind of care only a mother's hands know. She'd tucked a cereal bar in the front pocket "just in case," and kissed the top of his head three times before he left. "Make magic, darling. Just be yourself."

He carried those words like armour.

The first few sessions were electric. Warm-up games that made him laugh, group scenes that gave him goosebumps, older teens who clapped when he delivered his lines right. Felix felt seen in a way he hadn't in a long time, noticed for something other than being sensitive. He wasn't the weird kid here. He was just a kid who belonged.

There was a man there. Not the lead instructor, but someone who helped out, maybe late twenties, kind voice, the kind of adult who crouched when he talked to you. He remembered Felix's name on the second day. Said he had "stage presence." Gave him a nickname. Called him "Superstar."

Felix didn't know what fatherly love was supposed to feel like. But if it looked like someone calling you "Superstar" and saying, "I've got a good feeling about you," this must have been close.

So when that man offered to stay behind after rehearsal to help him with his solo scene, Felix said yes.
Eagerly.
Trustingly.
He was only a child.

What followed was confusion more than pain. A shifting of the atmosphere. A coldness that didn't match the warmth of everything before. The man's tone dropped. His touch lingered. His words blurred.

The world didn't split in two in that moment. It just… tilted. Just slightly.

He didn't understand what had happened. Not really. He didn't have the words. Only the feeling, one that crawled beneath his skin and told him something was wrong.

The man smiled and said, "Don't tell anyone. This is between us."
He made it sound like a compliment. Like Felix should feel special.

So Felix didn't tell.
Not for days.

Not for years.

Instead, he walked home with his script crumpled in his pocket and silence wrapped around his chest. He smiled for Begonia. Ate dinner without appetite. Watched his favourite Nickelodeon shows without laughter. Something inside him had shut off. Not broken exactly, just… paused.

He washed his own hoodie that night. Quietly. Even though Begonia always did that. He didn't want her to smell what had happened. Didn't want to bring anything home that might change how she looked at him.

The next morning, Begonia offered a full english breakfast. Felix's favourite, but he wasn't hungry. That was the first time she really looked at him. That kind of look only mothers give, the one that scans the soul and gently asks: "Are you okay, love?"

He nodded and said "I'm just tired."
She didn't push. But she didn't smile, either.

That night, Begonia tucked him in like she always did. Sat on the edge of his bed, ran her fingers through his hair. "You're safe, sweetheart," she whispered, almost as if she could sense he didn't believe it anymore.

At school, Felix grew quieter. Flinched a little when friends leaned too close. Laughed, but only when he had to. He dropped out of the stage group a week later. Said he "got bored of it." Lied without blinking.

He didn't know the term trauma yet.
He just knew something had happened that made him feel… wrong. Like maybe it was his fault.

Because that's what shame does to children, it teaches them to protect the person who hurt them before they even know what protection is.

And then, one day, Amber appeared.

Not in person. But on a television screen. Hair like sunlight. A voice
that soared. Eyes full of both glitter and ache. She sang like she knew
things. Like she'd been through things. Like she was reaching through
the screen and pulling him out.

Felix had never felt so seen.

He saved up for a CD, played it on loop and her voice filled the cracks
the silence had left behind. In the privacy of his room, he danced like
nothing had ever touched him. He mimed every word like it was a
prayer. He let the rhythm shake something loose, not the pain itself,
but the freeze.

Amber became his safe person.

She was everything he wasn't allowed to be, loud, free, bold,
unapologetically feeling.
And she never once told him to be quiet.

Through her, he didn't just survive, he created. Dance routines. Lip
syncs. Little skits he'd put on for himself in the mirror. And slowly, he
began to reclaim something.

He was still scared.
Still wounded.
Still carrying something he couldn't explain.

But he was also still here.
And somehow, that was enough.

CHAPTER FOUR

The Quiet Between the Acts

had always thought the stage was his sanctuary, a place where he could disappear into a role, even if only for a little while. But after months of pretending, forcing a confidence that didn't feel like his own, the weight of it all finally pressed down on him.

At the end of last year, he'd walked away from the stage group. Rehearsals had become more than practice, they were a performance of life itself, and he was tired of bending into someone else's expectations. The scripts, the lights, the applause faded into silence.

The quiet that followed wasn't peaceful. It was loud. It echoed in his room, in the hallways at school, in the pauses between conversations. Felix drifted through those days like a shadow of himself.

Food had become something he reached for almost automatically. Not hunger, exactly, more a small, urgent comfort. A few crisps after school, a chocolate bar snatched at night while the house was still, a nibble of cake left over from breakfast. It wasn't conscious, not fully; it was a fleeting relief, a way to fill a hollow space he couldn't name.

Begonia noticed, of course. She noticed the lingering glances, the way he sometimes lingered near the cupboards for no reason, the small crumbs he never quite hid. But she never pressed. She would leave a note tucked into his books, cook the meals he loved, sit nearby while he stared out the window. Her presence was quiet support, a soft anchor in his drifting days.

Amber's music remained his constant. Her new album played low as he rearranged his room, straightened posters, and quietly tested choreography in front of the mirror. Hairbrush in hand, he would sing along, eyes shut, imagining himself confident and seen, just for those few minutes, just for himself. It was ritual now, a lifeline.

Some evenings, he would pause in the kitchen, a small snack in hand, and watch the rain against the window. The sound of the droplets was like a metronome, a slow heartbeat that steadied him. He never lingered long. He never let it feel like indulgence. But the acts themselves, small, secret, deliberate, reminded him that he could make choices, even when the world felt unsteady.

Then came the note from Mr. Hayes, the drama teacher who had quietly admired his talent from afar:

"There's a new play starting next term. It's about finding your voice in a noisy world. We think you'd be perfect."

Felix held it in his hands for a long time. The stage was both a sanctuary and a place of scars. But something stirred, a quiet pulse of hope that maybe he could try again, not as a performance, but as himself.

Begonia saw the note too. She didn't push or plead. She simply said, "If you want to go back, I'll be there to watch you."

And that was enough.

That night, Felix lay awake, heart pounding with a strange mix of excitement and fear. The path ahead was uncertain, but for the first time in a long time, he felt like he was stepping into his own story, not just an actor playing a part, but a boy finding his voice.

Food still tugged at him sometimes, a quiet habit he barely acknowledged. A leftover cookie, a hidden chocolate bar, nothing dramatic, just the familiar tug that whispered for comfort when the world felt too loud. It wasn't hunger; it was a space-filler, a small ritual that made him feel he could control at least one thing in his life.

Amber's voice lingered in his mind as he turned over the day's events. Her songs had always reminded him he was seen, that he was capable of more than he often allowed himself to believe. Now, combined with the small victories on stage, her music became a soft guide, a promise that even when silence returned, he could carve his own rhythm in it.

For the first time in months, Felix felt a subtle shift: a spark of agency, a quiet assertion that he could be both careful and brave. And maybe, just maybe, he didn't have to vanish to survive anymore.

The next day, he would step back onto the stage again. But tonight, in the dark, he let himself breathe.

CHAPTER FIVE

Shadows and Light

Felix Asher was learning that healing didn't arrive in big, cinematic moments. It came in soft, stubborn flickers, moments when he chose to stay instead of vanish, when he dared to hope instead of hide.

After stepping back into the theatre group, something inside Felix began to thaw. The stage still made him nervous, the spotlight could feel like a heat lamp on old wounds, but it also made him feel real. There, he didn't have to be the version of himself that twisted and bent to please others. On stage, he was allowed to be fragile. And strong. And messy. And loud. All at once.

But that didn't mean things were easy.

School remained a daily minefield of awkward smiles and unsaid things. The people he used to feel closest to were shifting, like puzzle pieces that once fit but no longer clicked. The popular crowd (the one he'd once desperately tried to blend into) had started giving him strange looks again. One lunchtime, he overheard a boy whisper, "Why's he back in drama? Guess he finally gave up pretending." Laughter followed, and Felix shrunk inward like a snapped rubber band.

Even so, he said nothing. He just walked past, chewing the inside of his cheek and telling himself he didn't care.

But he did.

That evening, when Begonia had gone upstairs, the house fell silent, just the faint hum of the fridge and the whisper of wind brushing against the windows. That was when it usually happened. The ache. The pull. The need to fill an emptiness that had nothing to do with hunger.

He stood in the kitchen, staring at the cupboards as if they were calling to him. He opened one, then another, until his hands landed on whatever he could find, a family-sized bag of crisps, a half-empty box of biscuits, a bar of chocolate that wasn't even his. He ate fast, standing there in the dark. The taste didn't matter. The chewing did. Each crunch muted something in his head. Each handful quieted the noise for a moment, the loneliness, the guilt, the invisible heaviness that clung to him no matter how much he smiled in public.

He ate until the ache in his chest dulled into something else, shame.

Later, he sat on his bed in the dark, his stomach heavy and his heart heavier. His fingers brushed over the crumbs on his bedsheet. He hated himself for it, for needing food to cope, for the secret, for the loss of control. It became a cycle he couldn't name, but it had already started to tighten around him.

He'd stopped really looking in the mirror months ago. When he did, he barely recognised the boy staring back. His face had softened. His clothes fit differently. He would pull at the fabric, turning sideways, searching for something that used to be there. The comparison crept in, to the boys at school with their sharp jawlines and easy confidence. He wondered if they ever felt this way. If they ever looked in the mirror and flinched.

But deep down, Felix knew it wasn't just about food. It was about control. About trying to fill a space that had been left hollow since childhood, the part of him that had been made to feel wrong, different, unworthy. He didn't have anyone to measure himself against growing up. Just that silent question in his head: Why am I like this?

And then there was Amber.

Amber was the one light that never flickered. Her new album had just dropped, every song like a diary entry written for him. Track three, "Brighter Than Before," became his quiet obsession. The lyrics sank beneath his skin:

"You're not broken, just bruised

You're not lost, just waiting to be found…"

He played it over and over, his voice whispering along under his breath. Sometimes he'd stand in front of the mirror and sing with her, eyes closed, hairbrush in hand, pretending for those three minutes that he belonged somewhere. That he was someone worth seeing.

In those moments, his reflection didn't disgust him. It softened. The boy in the glass became someone he could almost love, someone Amber might sing to. She made him feel different for all the right reasons, like maybe the things that set him apart weren't curses after all, but clues to something extraordinary.

The fantasy of his bedroom became his stage. His escape. His confession.

One Sunday morning, as the sky outside turned the colour of ash, Begonia knocked on his door with a cup of tea and a soft, sleepy smile.

"You've barely touched your breakfast," she said gently. "You okay?"

He hesitated, then nodded. "Just tired."

Begonia didn't push. Instead, she sat down at the edge of his bed and placed the mug in his hands. "I know school's hard. And life's loud right now. But you're not alone in it."

He felt the words hit somewhere deep. "I don't think I even know who I am anymore."

She smiled, not with pity, but with that rare understanding only a mother could offer. "That's because you're still becoming him."

Felix blinked, holding back a sudden wave of tears.

"You're allowed to not have it figured out," she added. "You're growing through things most people will never understand. That's your strength, Felix. Not your weakness."

Later that week, rehearsals shifted something again.

The play was about a boy who lost his voice and had to fight to get it back. Felix had been cast as the lead, something that terrified him and thrilled him in equal measure. But as the director read through the script, line by line, Felix started to feel something he hadn't in a long time:

Seen.

There was a monologue in Act Two, a raw, vulnerable moment where the character confesses everything he's afraid to say out loud. As Felix rehearsed it, his hands shook. His voice cracked. The words felt far too close to home.

When he finished, there was silence in the room.

Then applause.

Not the loud, performative kind. A soft, stunned kind, real, honest, human. Even the director had mist in his eyes.

Felix sat down afterward, heart pounding. And in that moment, he realised something: he didn't just love acting because it let him escape. He loved it because it let him tell the truth, even when he couldn't speak it as himself.

And maybe… just maybe… that was enough.

Or at least, it had to be. Because when the lights dimmed, and the applause faded, and he was alone again, the silence crept back in.

The same silence that hummed between every heartbeat. The kind that made him wonder if he'd ever really be loved for who he was.

He didn't know it yet, but that question, that quiet ache, was about to be answered.
Not by the stage.
Not by Amber's voice
But by someone unexpected.

Someone whose arrival would change everything.

CHAPTER SIX

Threads of Truth

The final months of Felix's school days hung heavy with a strange mix of anticipation and exhaustion. Each morning felt like stepping onto a stage set with shifting lights, he knew his lines, but the script was growing harder to follow. The mask he wore was becoming heavier, and the applause quieter. The popular crowd he'd longed to join was a dazzling but distant world, and Felix realised that no matter how hard he tried, he was still an outsider looking in.

Cherry had been there all along, weaving quietly through the crowded hallways and bustling classrooms. She was part of the popular group Felix had craved so hard to be around, loud laughter, effortless charm, a confidence that seemed unshakable. But beneath the surface, Cherry was struggling with her own secret: she had been pretending to be someone she wasn't, caught in the glittering web of expectations and whispers.

It was during one of those dull, grey autumn afternoons, the kind that made the world feel like it was holding its breath, that Cherry appeared in a way that would change everything. Not with fanfare or drama, but simply, quietly, like a sudden breath of fresh air. Her hair caught the weak sunlight as she walked down the corridor, laughter bubbling up effortlessly, unrestrained. Felix noticed her immediately, not because she was loud or flashy, but because she seemed utterly unbothered by the invisible walls others built around themselves.

Their meeting was almost accidental but perfectly fitting, both had chosen textiles art as an elective, a rare shared interest in a school that often seemed designed to spotlight what made them different. Felix found comfort in the textures and colours, the tactile nature of fabric a quiet contrast to the noise of everyday life. Cherry approached the project table with an easy confidence, her eyes bright with curiosity.

"Hey, I'm Cherry," she said, offering a hand with a smile that didn't ask for anything but gave so much in return.

Felix hesitated, heart thumping fiercely, before shaking it. The warmth from her touch was unexpected. They began working side by side, threading needles, experimenting with patterns, sharing thoughts on design choices and favourite music. Cherry's enthusiasm was contagious, breaking down the walls Felix had carefully constructed.

Slowly, the barrier between them began to crumble. They talked about everything, the pressure of fitting in, the loneliness of hiding one's true self. Cherry confessed her own fear of losing her identity in the popular crowd, while Felix revealed the heaviness of always wearing a mask, afraid of being truly seen.

But beneath those conversations, Felix was fighting something deeper. A truth that had been quietly growing inside him since childhood, confusing and terrifying all at once.

He had never been able to say it aloud, not even to himself. The way his chest fluttered around certain boys, the way he'd noticed details others seemed to overlook, the shape of a smile, the way a voice could sound softer when directed at him. It wasn't the same as the crushes his friends talked about. It was something quieter, heavier. Something that made him feel both alive and ashamed.

He'd spent years convincing himself it would fade. That it was just a phase. That he'd meet a girl one day and it would all make sense. But deep down, it never did.

And then there was Geo.

He wasn't in Felix's circle, more of a familiar face from another class, but he carried something magnetic about him. Maybe it was his calmness, or the confidence in the way he spoke to teachers without shrinking. Maybe it was the way his laughter filled the corridor like music. Whatever it was, Felix noticed him more than he meant to.

The first time Geo caught his eye and smiled, Felix's stomach dropped. He didn't understand how one simple look could unravel him so completely. It wasn't even romantic in the way movies showed it. It was just… a feeling. A pulse that told him he wasn't broken. That the part of him he'd buried might actually be something real.

But the realisation scared him.

That night, Felix stood in front of the mirror, gripping the sink, staring at his reflection. He studied his rounder face, the softness he hated, the way he always looked slightly out of place in his own skin. He compared himself to the boys at school, tall, lean, effortlessly confident. He didn't see himself in them. He didn't see himself anywhere.

He whispered the truth into the empty bathroom. "I'm gay."

The words echoed, unfamiliar and fragile. For a moment, he hated himself for saying it. Then, just as quickly, he felt something else. Relief.

It didn't fix everything. But it was the first thread of honesty he'd dared to pull.

One chilly afternoon, with golden leaves tumbling past the classroom window, Felix found the courage to share a piece of that truth with Cherry. They were the last two left in the art room, their fingers stained with dye and glue, the silence between them charged with possibility.

"I… I haven't told many people this," Felix began, voice barely above a whisper. His hands trembled as he fiddled with a loose thread on his jacket. "But I think I'm gay. I mean, I am gay. I just don't know how to feel okay about it yet."

Cherry looked up, her gaze steady and patient. "You can tell me anything."

He swallowed hard. "It's not something I'm proud of yet. Not because of who I am… but because I'm scared. Scared of the whispers, the judgment, the disgust I feel bubbling up inside me every time I think about it."

The silence that followed was thick, heavy, a breath held too long. Felix's heart thundered in his ears, his skin prickling with shame and vulnerability. For a moment, he wanted nothing more than to take it all back.

But then Cherry reached out, her hand warm and steady, squeezing his gently.

"Thank you for trusting me with that," she said softly. "You don't have to be afraid with me. You're Felix, and that's more than enough. Always."

Her words broke something open. Relief mingled with a fragile, unfamiliar hope. For the first time, Felix felt seen, not as a character playing a role, but as the real person beneath.

Days turned into weeks, and their friendship blossomed into something deeper. They met outside class, at the quiet library tucked away at the back of the school, a sanctuary from the noise. They traded music and stories, Cherry's playlists opening new worlds to Felix, while his tales found a listener who didn't flinch or turn away.

He told her about Geo once, tentatively, how there was something about him that made his heart race. Cherry just smiled knowingly, as if she'd already guessed. "That's what it's supposed to feel like," she said.

Felix didn't respond, but that night he lay awake replaying that sentence. That's what it's supposed to feel like.

And for the first time, he didn't feel wrong.

One evening, after a day heavy with unspoken worries, Felix wandered to the old park near his house. The sky was painted in fading purples and golds, the cool air sharp against his skin. Sitting on a worn bench, he tried to make sense of the storm inside.

Cherry appeared beside him without a word, offering a steaming cup of hot chocolate. The warmth seeped into his cold fingers as she said quietly, "You don't have to carry it all on your own."

For the first time in years, Felix let his guard fall. He spoke haltingly of the loneliness that shadowed him since childhood, the nights wrestling with thoughts no one else could understand, the pressure to be someone he wasn't. Cherry listened, eyes steady and kind, a harbour in the storm.

When he finished, she smiled. "You're stronger than you think. And you don't have to prove it to anyone."

The school halls, once cold and oppressive, softened around the edges. Felix felt, perhaps for the first time, that he might survive this chapter, and maybe, just maybe, thrive in the next.

And somewhere in that softening, in the spaces between his laughter and Cherry's light, Geo's name began to echo in the back of his mind, not as confusion anymore, but as truth.

CHAPTER SEVEN

The Summer Between

Felix's room had always been a place of quiet order. Every poster perfectly aligned, each CD in its rightful place, mostly Amber albums, arranged chronologically like sacred texts. The soft blue glow of fairy lights illuminated shelves filled with neatly stacked *Top of the Pops* magazines, childhood mementos, and a few hand-painted canvases he'd never dared show anyone but Cherry. His room wasn't just a space; it was a sanctuary, somewhere the world couldn't find him unless he wanted it to.

Cherry had become a regular presence there, often sprawled across his floor with her shoes kicked off, flipping through Felix's photo albums. She'd grin at him from beneath a wall of Amber posters and tease, "Alright, what's the latest masterpiece you're forcing me to watch today?"

He'd roll his eyes playfully and hit play on the music video of the week. Amber in high-definition, all glitter and choreography, her voice rising above heartbreaks and headlines. Felix would watch Cherry's expression as much as the screen, needing her to see what he saw: a woman who survived, who shined anyway.

"You're obsessed," Cherry would laugh, but never unkindly.

"She gets it," Felix would reply quietly.

And Cherry did. There was comfort in their rituals, dancing in socks on the hardwood floor, mouthing lyrics into hairbrushes, dissecting performances like scholars. In those moments, the heaviness Felix often carried seemed to lift.

Outside those four walls, the world was shifting. The end of school was creeping closer like a sunset on fast-forward. Teachers were distracted, lockers were clearing, and the scent of old textbooks and anticipation filled the air.

Their final summer as school kids unfolded differently than they'd imagined. Gone were the cliché teen movie scenes of parties and beach trips. Instead, their time together was wrapped in gentler, more meaningful adventures.

There were countless coffee trips, cheap lattes in corner cafés where they'd claim a window seat and talk for hours. Conversations bounced between dreams of the future and reflections of a past they weren't ready to let go of.

But it was the charity shop days that Felix treasured most.

They'd wander through musty little stores tucked into quiet streets, rifling through bins of old toys, scratched DVDs, faded T-shirts with long-forgotten slogans. For Felix, each discovery was like unearthing a piece of himself. A Spice Girls lunchbox. A Beanie Baby missing an eye. A VHS of a cartoon he hadn't thought about in years. He'd cradle the objects like relics, reluctant to leave them behind.

"I'm scared to forget," he admitted once, holding up a battered children's book he hadn't seen since nursery.

"You don't have to," Cherry said, gently taking it from his hands. "Some things are worth carrying with you."

They bought far too much, trinkets, mugs with chipped edges, a cassette player with no guarantee of working. But it wasn't really about the items. It was about preserving a feeling, anchoring themselves to something real while the ground shifted beneath them.

Back in Felix's room, the new treasures found their place among the old. It became their ritual: unpacking the day's finds, playing songs on repeat, and laughing about nothing at all.

And slowly, between the laughter and the stillness, something inside Felix began to change.

He had spent years hiding from himself, from the truth that had once frightened him into silence. But now, with Cherry's kindness steady beside him, he was beginning to see it differently.

He *was* gay. And for the first time, that didn't feel like something to be ashamed of. It was simply a part of him, quiet, steady, waiting to be accepted.

That realisation came fully into focus the day he OFFICIALLY met Geo.

It happened at a friend-of-a-friend's gathering in the park, one of those long summer evenings that stretched lazily into dusk. Someone had brought speakers, and pop songs drifted through the air, mingling with the scent of cut grass and barbecue smoke. Felix had gone reluctantly, expecting awkward small talk and the familiar ache of not quite fitting in.

Then he saw him.

Geo.

He wasn't the loudest in the group or the one everyone looked at first. He was leaning against a tree, half-listening to the conversation, sunlight catching the sharpness of his perfectly styled hair. There was an ease about him, a stillness that felt rare. When he laughed, his whole face transformed, unguarded and sincere.

Felix felt it instantly, that spark. The first real one since Clarke. It startled him, the way it filled his chest like a held breath.

They spoke briefly when Geo asked to borrow his lighter for the small fire someone had started. Their hands brushed, and Felix's heart reacted before his brain could catch up. They talked about music, of course they did, and when Geo mentioned that he loved Amber too, Felix laughed, unable to hide his disbelief.

"No one ever says that," he grinned.

Geo shrugged, smiling. "She's real. And I like real."

Felix didn't have an answer for that. He just stared a moment too long, memorising the way Geo's eyes glinted in the fading light.

But then someone called Geo's name, and just like that, he was gone. A fleeting moment, the kind that didn't feel accidental.

That night, Felix replayed it all on loop. The brush of fingers, the sound of Geo's voice, the look that felt like recognition. He didn't tell Cherry about it at first. He wanted to keep it to himself, this small spark that felt like proof that he *could* still feel something beautiful and good.

But along with that new awareness came something darker, the desperate need for control.

He started exercising more, watching what he ate, tracking every bite, every movement. It began innocently enough, a promise to feel healthier, to feel *better.* But it quickly became something else. Each night without fail, he'd put on one of Amber's fitness DVDs, following every move with disciplined precision. It had to be *her*, of course. It was always Amber who guided him through the hardest things.

As the weight dropped off, the compliments started.
"You look incredible."
"You've never looked better."
"You've changed so much!"

At first, those words felt like fuel. Proof that he was finally becoming someone worthy of being seen, someone who might deserve a Geo, or anyone. But the more people praised his changing body, the more he began to resent their words.

Because when people say *you look amazing* after you've changed, what they're really saying is *you weren't enough before.*

And that thought cut deeper than anyone could see.

He replaced one eating disorder with another, without even realising it. The control became addictive. The smaller he got, the more trapped he felt. Mirrors became both comfort and punishment. Even when his clothes hung loose, he couldn't see what others saw. He still felt ugly.

Still felt not enough.

And yet, amid all that confusion, light kept finding its way back in. In Cherry's laughter. In Amber's lyrics. In the quiet replay of Geo's smile.

There was one night in particular that lingered, late July, thunder rumbling low in the distance, the smell of rain clinging to the air. They were curled up on beanbags, sharing a blanket and a bar of half-melted chocolate. Amber's live performance from Paris played quietly in the background.

Cherry leaned her head on his shoulder. "You're going to be okay, you know."

Felix swallowed hard. "You think?"

"I know," she said. "You're Felix Asher. There's a light in you, even when you can't see it."

And for the first time in a long while, he believed her, not completely, but enough. Enough to keep trying. Enough to believe that maybe, just maybe, who he was becoming wasn't something to hide anymore.

CHAPTER EIGHT

The End of the Beginning

The final bell didn't sound like freedom. It sounded like falling.

When it echoed through the corridors, it should have meant celebration, the end of years spent pretending, surviving, holding his breath. But for Felix, it rang hollow. The sound lingered in the air like a question he wasn't ready to answer.

No one cried, no one clung to lockers whispering promises to stay in touch. Just the scrape of chairs, the slam of lockers, the faint smell of disinfectant on desks that had seen too much of everyone's mess. It was an ending without ceremony, the kind Felix had grown used to.

He stayed behind, fingertips tracing carved initials in the desk, the peeling posters on the walls. His reflection caught in a framed photo from the school play three years ago, a younger Felix, mid-laugh on stage. But the smile looked like armour. The kind you wear to survive a battlefield disguised as adolescence.

Outside, Cherry waited, leaning against the gate like she had all the time in the world. She didn't greet him with noise or fuss, just a quiet, steady look that said *I see you.*

"You okay?" she asked softly.

He nodded. "I think so."

They walked home together, their steps falling in rhythm, the kind of silence between them that wasn't empty, just unspoken understanding.

That summer should have tasted like freedom, but it didn't. It was soft and uncertain, like the morning fog that never quite lifts.

Without routines or rules, Felix filled his days with nostalgia, maybe to keep from slipping into the unknown. He and Cherry drifted through charity shops and record stalls, fingers brushing across forgotten CDs, sticker albums, and the worn-out toys of childhood.

Felix was searching for fragments of himself. Every memory, every relic of who he used to be.
Cherry watched him cradle an old Amber: Live in Las Vegas DVD as if it were sacred.

"You ever think you're trying to trap the past in your pocket?" she asked.

He looked down. "Maybe I'm scared I'll forget who I was, before I started pretending."

That truth lingered in the air, fragile and freeing all at once.

They'd follow those afternoons with coffee runs, Cherry ordering something overly complicated, Felix with his simple white Americano and a wink: "Hold the sugar, I'm sweet enough."

She'd laugh, make him try her drink, and he'd pull a face every time. But beneath their laughter was an unspoken fear: that this chapter of their lives was already fading.

Felix's bedroom became their world, their safe little universe where everything made sense.

Amber's face stared down from the walls in every era of her life, fairy lights glowed softly over the desk, and his CD collection lined the shelves like trophies. It wasn't just decoration, it was identity. Proof he'd survived.

Sometimes Cherry sprawled across his neatly made bed, half-listening as he played her music videos and explained the deeper meaning behind Amber's lyrics. She teased him for being "emotionally invested," but she never really joked when she said it. She knew it was more than fandom, it was faith.

Then came the letter.

It sat unopened on his dresser for days. A place on a Creative Arts course, the kind of dream he'd once thought belonged to other people. When he finally let Cherry read it, they sat in the glow of fairy lights, Amber's voice humming low through the speakers.

"This is huge," Cherry whispered.

"I don't know if I'm brave enough," he admitted.

She smiled gently. "You don't have to be brave all the time. But you do need to be honest about what you want. And Felix, your life isn't meant to stay small."

Her words sank deep. He looked around his perfectly ordered room and realised, it wasn't comfort anymore. It was safety disguised as stillness.

The last weeks of summer became their long goodbye.

They recorded voice notes for the future, shared melting ice creams, and sketched dream wardrobes on the backs of receipts. Felix opened up more than ever, about the years of shame, the cruelty he'd endured, and the nights he'd cried himself hollow.

Cherry listened. She didn't interrupt. Didn't tell him to move on. Just placed a hand over his and said, "You're not broken. You've just been made to feel that way."

Her words stitched something back together in him, something fragile but real.

By September, the world felt different.

Felix's days began to scatter, a job here, a course there, a few new faces that never quite stuck. He even started speaking more to people. One of them was Geo.

At first, Geo felt like a small miracle, funny, sharp, a little too confident but always present. They talked every day, their conversations stretching into the early hours. Geo made Felix feel seen, but in a way that slowly began to twist. Compliments came laced with control; warmth came with conditions. When Felix didn't reply fast enough, the tone would shift, playful teasing turning into guilt.

It was confusing. Geo could be kind, even protective, but there was always a current of possession underneath. What started as friendship blurred into something that looked like affection but felt like imbalance.

And Felix, desperate to be wanted, tried to ignore the knots forming in his stomach.

He met a few others too, small flares of interest that burned out quickly. They smiled, they flirted, but none made him feel what he was searching for. None of them had *that spark*, the one he'd always imagined love would feel like, not fireworks, but warmth. Not obsession, but home.

Some nights, lying awake, he wondered if people like him ever really found it. Maybe love only belonged to the ones who fit, the ones the world made room for.

Still, he hoped.

Because somewhere deep inside, Felix Asher refused to give up on the idea that love could be gentle, that it could arrive when he least expected it, and not ask him to shrink in order to be chosen.

He didn't know it yet, but his next chapter was already on its way.

And one evening soon, in a dimly lit car park, everything he thought he knew about love was going to change forever.

CHAPTER NINE

Turning Points and First Glimmers

The days after school ended pressed down on Felix like thick fog. While his classmates buzzed with excitement, creative arts courses, fresh starts, new cities, he felt a hollow weight in his chest. The world beyond home felt vast, unpredictable, and somehow unwelcoming.

Night after restless night, he wrestled with a quiet decision: he would turn down the creative arts course. Not because he lacked talent or passion, but because he wasn't ready to leave the fragile safety of home. The thought of leaving the sanctuary of his perfectly ordered room, the familiar scent of Amber's CDs and posters surrounding him like old friends, made the future feel like a storm he couldn't navigate.

Life slowed into a quieter rhythm. Felix filled his days with small, deliberate pieces of art, part-time work, and online courses, threading his creativity into safe, manageable pockets. Evenings were structured, almost ritualistic. He followed Amber's fitness DVD without fail, a single hour to push his body while the music drowned out the spiralling thoughts in his head. Compliments came, people noticed his changing shape, but he barely heard them. Mirrors still reflected someone he didn't recognise, someone too small, too sharp-edged, still flawed in his own eyes.

Cherry remained his anchor. Her laughter and presence pulled him from the edges of his own isolation. They spent hours together, sprawled across his bed, arguing playfully over Amber's choreography, or dissecting music videos with a meticulous devotion that felt like both ritual and refuge. Felix's room, every poster, every CD, every carefully curated detail, became a cocoon he could share only with those who understood him.

And then there was Geo.
Geo had left Felix with an unfamiliar flutter, a spark he hadn't felt in years. But in the weeks that followed, he began noticing the edges that didn't fit: the way Geo sometimes joked at others' expense and the way conversations always seemed to revolve around him. It wasn't

unpleasant, he enjoyed Geo's charm, but it didn't feel like the quiet, consuming warmth Felix longed for.

Even as he lingered over memories of that park day, Felix found himself reflecting on what he wanted, and what he didn't. Some days, he allowed himself to hope; other days, he noticed the hollowness behind the charm. The lessons of past crushes and fleeting attractions were not wasted: he was learning to discern what mattered, to notice the difference between excitement and depth.

The summer ahead promised nothing certain, yet Felix felt a subtle pull, a whisper of possibility he hadn't dared to entertain before. With Cherry's unwavering presence at his side, he began to imagine that maybe, just maybe, he could step beyond the edges of his world.

He still spent hours in his room, relishing its quiet order, the scent of sea salt and lavender filling the air. He made space for laughter, for music, for small, shared secrets. These moments were his own, and they reminded him that life could be more than a string of shadows.

As he wandered the buzzing streets of London with Cherry, or caught films in darkened cinemas where the flickering light mirrored unspoken stirrings in his heart, Felix felt something awaken. A delicate hope, fragile and trembling, that a connection he had never dared to believe in might finally find him.

He was still discovering himself, his desires, his boundaries, the way his body and his mind intersected, but he had begun to see that he was allowed to want more than just safety. That he was allowed to feel butterflies. That he could let someone in, even cautiously.

It was only a beginning, subtle, almost imperceptible, but it was enough to make him notice that the world, for the first time in a long time, might be ready to tilt just a little in his favour.

CHAPTER TEN

Shadowboxing

Felix had always imagined that when school ended, freedom would feel like sunlight, sharp, clear, and full of promise. But instead, it arrived like mist. Soft. Hesitant. Impossible to grasp.

The weight of those long years didn't disappear overnight. The halls he once wandered became ghosts in his mind, and the boy who had tried so hard to blend in was slowly fading into someone quieter, more deliberate.

He had been offered a place on the creative arts course, a golden ticket he once would have grabbed without question. But when the moment came, he couldn't bring himself to go. He wasn't ready to perform again, even creatively. He was done proving himself to anyone.

So instead, he rented a small room above a corner shop. Barely enough for a bed and a desk, but it was his. Warm, earthy tones on the walls. Photos, postcards, ticket stubs, and the first candle he'd ever made filled the space. Sea salt and lavender. The scent reminded him to breathe.

The first few weeks were quiet, sometimes too quiet. The hum of traffic below replaced the clink of cups and his mother's morning radio. Freedom, it turned out, could be a lonely sound.

Cherry visited often, grounding him with her usual spark. Coffee, gossip, and laughter that shook the dust off his walls. They sprawled across his bed, dissecting Amber's choreography, arguing over music videos, laughing until their sides hurt. His room, perfectly ordered, scented, safe, became their shared cocoon, the one place he could exhale.

But beneath it all, Felix carried an ache he didn't speak of. Love, real, lasting love, had always felt like something for other people. He'd seen too many almosts, too many false starts that crumbled before they began. People loved him in fragments, never fully.

Geo had once stirred something inside him, a connection he hadn't felt since Clarke. But the spark had faded. Their friendship now carried an unease, small cuts of tension wrapped in Geo's charm. He liked to be the centre of attention, and Felix had learned to orbit carefully, knowing exactly where the boundaries lay.

Then Ethan appeared in a way that made Felix's stomach flutter. One evening, his phone buzzed with a new message notification. It was from Ethan.

Hey, I saw your post about the Amber video… you have great taste. Thought I'd say hi.

Felix stared at the screen, his fingers trembling slightly. His heart raced faster than he thought possible. He typed, deleted, retyped, then finally sent a reply. A few messages later, the conversation was flowing, easy and teasing, like they had known each other far longer than they had. Every ping of the phone brought a little thrill, a little hope he hadn't dared to feel in years.

The next day, sitting across from Geo at their usual café after running errands, Felix could hardly contain his excitement.

"You won't believe this," he said, practically bouncing in his seat. "Ethan messaged me. Like, directly. On his own. Can you believe it?"

Geo raised an eyebrow, a small smirk tugging at the corner of his lips. "Mm. Interesting." He leaned back in his chair, arms crossed, his eyes sharp. "You and Ethan wouldn't work. He's… complicated, and you wouldn't want to get a name for yourself now would you?"

Felix's excitement faltered slightly. "Why? What do you mean?"

Geo just shrugged, muttering something about "protecting the dynamic," as if that explained everything.

The truth was simpler, Geo liked being the one people wanted. He liked the attention Ethan gave him, the easy flirtation that never quite crossed a line. But when Ethan's focus shifted to Felix, it exposed something ugly in him, possessiveness wrapped in false concern.

For the first time, Felix saw through it. And for once, he didn't listen.

Ethan and Felix began talking privately. Long conversations that started light but soon turned into something deeper. They spoke about fears, about past mistakes, about the small things that made them who they were. There was a tenderness in Ethan's words, a patience that felt unfamiliar.

And so, one evening, against Geo's warning, they agreed to meet.

Felix arrived early, standing in the cool breath of a dimly lit petrol station car park just off the A-road. His hands shook, half from nerves and half from disbelief. The world felt both enormous and small all at once. He didn't think anyone would ever *choose* to see him like this, stripped of profile pictures and typed-out confidence.

Then headlights cut through the dark.

The car that pulled in was low and fast, the kind that hummed with quiet confidence. The door opened, and Ethan stepped out.

He was slightly older, maybe by a couple of years, with short, styled hair and an effortless cool that didn't feel forced. Slightly shorter than Felix, broader across the shoulders, he had a grounded presence, the kind that made you feel steady just by standing near him.

"Felix?" Ethan said, smiling.

And just like that, something in Felix's chest loosened.

They sat in Ethan's car for hours, the soft hum of the radio filling the spaces between words. They traded songs, shared stories, and laughed over nothing. The world outside didn't exist, just the faint glow of the dashboard, the rhythm of their voices, and the quiet realisation that something had shifted.

When Ethan leaned in, it wasn't rehearsed. It wasn't movie-perfect. It was clumsy, shy, real. The kiss tasted faintly of mint and nerves. Felix felt the world stop spinning for just long enough to understand what it meant to be truly seen.

He thought of his favourite love story, *Titanic,* Jack and Rose, two worlds colliding against all odds. Maybe that's what this was: two souls meeting at the edge of something fragile and infinite.

Cherry noticed the change almost immediately. Felix's eyes carried a new light, soft but certain. They still met for coffee and walks through London, but now there was always a quiet smile tugging at his lips, like he was living in a secret he couldn't quite believe.

But that secret wasn't meant to stay hidden for long.

Geo found out.

It happened by accident, a photo on Felix's story, a fleeting reflection in a café window that Ethan hadn't even realised he was in. Within an hour, Geo's message flashed across Felix's phone.

"So you met him anyway?"

Felix stared at the screen, the words pulsing like static. He typed a reply, then deleted it. Then another.

"Yeah," he finally wrote. *"We did."*

The typing bubbles came and went. Then Geo's response landed like a stone.

"You really don't listen, do you?"

Felix felt that old sting, the quiet guilt of disappointing someone who had learned how to make him feel small. But this time, something inside him shifted.

He set the phone down.
He didn't explain himself.
He didn't apologise.

For once, he refused to shrink.

Later that night, Ethan messaged him.

"You okay?"

Felix hesitated, then smiled faintly. *"Yeah. For the first time in a while... I think I am."*

As he turned off the light, the lavender candle flickered beside him, sea salt and calm. Freedom didn't always roar. Sometimes, it whispered.

And this time, it whispered his name.

CHAPTER ELEVEN

A Love That Didn't Ask for Applause

The weeks that followed didn't feel like a whirlwind, they felt like a quiet exhale.

Felix had expected the start of something new to be chaotic, but instead, it was gentle. There was peace in the rhythm of independence, morning coffee, music humming through his small room, texts from Ethan that arrived just when he needed them most.

Geo's silence lingered like a shadow. He still appeared in group chats now and then, tossing out comments that seemed harmless on the surface, *"You've changed,"* or *"Don't forget who was there first."* But Felix could read between the lines. They weren't reminders; they were attempts to pull him back.

He tried to ignore it, though sometimes the guilt crept in, the way it always had when people made him feel like he'd taken up too much space. But Ethan never fed that insecurity. When Felix seemed distracted, Ethan didn't demand explanations; he just reached out and grounded him.

"Whoever's trying to make you feel small," Ethan said once, "they're just scared you're finally standing tall."

The words stuck.

Ethan was different from anyone Felix had known. He didn't ask for performances or perfection. He was just *there,* steady, grounded, and entirely present.

They spent hours walking along Southbank, drifting through tourist attractions and riverside cafés. They laughed about everything and nothing, took photographs of moments that didn't need capturing, and talked about their dreams in the kind of unguarded way you only can when you finally feel safe.

Felix often thought about how impossible it once felt, the idea that someone could want him just as he was. He had built walls, high and sturdy, convincing himself that love was something that happened to other people. But Ethan had walked right through them, not with force, but with kindness.

Their first kiss replayed in his mind like a favourite scene. Sometimes he'd catch himself smiling at the memory, the smell of leather, the hum of the engine, the way Ethan had whispered, *"It doesn't have to end."*

It hadn't.

Now, Ethan often stayed over. Felix's small room, once a symbol of solitude, became a shared space filled with laughter, music, and the warmth of two people figuring each other out. Ethan would lie back on the bed as Felix played Amber's latest video on repeat.

"Again?" Ethan would tease.

Felix would grin. "It's art. You wouldn't understand."

But Ethan always watched. Every time.

Their love didn't need grand gestures. It lived in the quiet things, the touch of a hand, the shared silence between songs, the gentle way Ethan said Felix's name like it was something to be cared for.

Geo lingered on the edges, not fully gone, not fully present. Sometimes, late at night, a message would appear: *"Hope he's worth it."* And Felix would look at the words, then at Ethan sleeping beside him, the soft rhythm of his breath steady in the dark.

He'd smile to himself, and type back only once.

"He is."

One afternoon, sunlight spilled across the bed, painting everything in gold. Felix turned to Ethan, his voice barely above a whisper.

"Do you think this could be something?"

Ethan reached out, brushing a stray hair from Felix's forehead. "I think it already is."

For once, Felix didn't question it. He simply believed.

Because this time, love didn't ask for applause, it just asked to be real.

And as he watched Ethan's steady breathing that evening, Felix realised that believing was only the first step. To let love in meant opening himself fully, letting the quiet warmth between them shape his days, his choices, and even his fears. Something deep inside him stirred, anticipation, hope, and the first flicker of courage to trust not just the magic of meeting someone, but the reality of being with them.

CHAPTER TWELVE

"What If It's Real?"

The warmth of summer had slipped quietly into early autumn, brushing the city with a new kind of hush, cooler mornings, gold-dusted trees, and shadows that stretched longer in the late afternoon light. Felix felt the change not just in the air, but in himself. The world around him seemed softer somehow, quieter, and he realised that he was seeing it through a different lens, one shaped by Ethan's presence, gentle yet insistent, colouring ordinary days with something like possibility.

It wasn't fireworks and chaos. It wasn't dramatic declarations or sweeping gestures. Their relationship had taken root quietly, almost secretly, like a tree strengthening its roots in silence. Felix could feel it, steady and alive beneath his skin. But with comfort came a whisper of fear he couldn't quite shake. What if it was real? What if it lasted? What if it changed him in ways he wasn't ready for?

"What if it's real?" he asked Cherry one afternoon, the two of them curled into the battered leather sofa of a quiet café tucked behind a second-hand bookshop. Rain tapped lightly against the windows, a rhythmic, soothing sound.

Cherry glanced at him, stirring her drink with a half-smile. "What if it is?"

Felix bit his lip. "That scares me more than if it wasn't."

She didn't laugh or try to dismiss it. Instead, she reached over, squeezing his hand gently. "Of course it does. Because real things mean something. But that doesn't make them wrong."

Her words lingered in his mind as he walked home later, crunching through leaves dampened by drizzle. He noticed the little things about Ethan: the crinkle at the corner of his eyes when he laughed, the careless flick of a hand, the way he hummed quietly when he thought no one was watching. These small gestures reminded Felix that love wasn't always loud; sometimes it existed in the softest, most overlooked moments.

They met often, sometimes without plans, just to exist together. Felix loved these quiet moments: making tea for two, watching obscure films while Ethan leaned against the counter scrolling through messages, half-listening but entirely present. Even Amber's music videos became shared rituals, Felix dissecting every outfit and choreography, Ethan watching patiently, teasing only occasionally.

"You know, I think you're rubbing off on me," Ethan said one evening, laughing as Felix launched into a monologue about a 2001 music video.

"You're welcome," Felix replied, grinning.

But amidst the laughter, there were small moments that gnawed at him. Sometimes Ethan's smiles felt distant, a little absent, as if a part of him were elsewhere. Texts sometimes went unanswered longer than expected. A casual brush of the hand or a delayed response sent Felix's mind spiralling into questions he couldn't always voice. Ethan was warm, attentive, funny, but there were shadows he couldn't quite reach.

Felix hated to admit it, but the uncertainty tugged at him. It wasn't fear of losing Ethan entirely, not yet. It was the quiet doubt that sometimes lingered when someone you cared for gave mixed signals, moments that were open, yet slightly closed, tender yet uncommitted. He found himself analysing every word, every gesture, trying to read meaning where there might not be any.

Their adventures continued: Camden Market, hidden museums, narrow streets lined with forgotten history. Ethan indulged Felix's obsessions with old tins and VHS tapes. Felix, in turn, began noticing subtle tensions, Ethan sometimes drifted in conversation, or hesitated before answering questions about the future. Nothing dramatic, but enough to make Felix's heart twitch with awareness.

Back in Felix's room, time felt suspended in the sanctuary he had built: Amber CDs stacked, posters pinned, wax melts lingering like memory. It was a world ordered to his taste, yet now inhabited by someone unpredictable. Ethan adapted, but sometimes the slight distance in his eyes reminded Felix that love could be thrilling and terrifying in the same breath.

They laughed a lot. Felix hadn't realised how much laughter had been missing until it became normal again. Yet he had to remind himself: warmth didn't erase complexity. Love wasn't a guarantee; it was a choice, moment by moment.

One rainy evening, under the duvet with the city breathing quietly outside, Ethan asked, "Have you told anyone else about me?"

The question landed like a stone in Felix's chest. Protecting himself had been second nature. "Cherry knows," he admitted. "And I think my mum suspects. But… it's hard."

Ethan's thumb traced slow circles on his hand. "You don't owe anyone anything you're not ready for. But just know, I don't want to be a secret forever."

Felix nodded. The honesty stung, not because Ethan was wrong, but because he was right. He wanted to trust him completely, yet old fears curled around new beginnings, whispering doubt into the quiet.

Gradually, Felix allowed himself to open more fully. Small details first, how Ethan liked his tea, his wrong lyrics, the subtle warmth of his hand. Then larger truths: how safe he felt in Ethan's presence, how scary it was to imagine losing that peace, how the mixed signals sometimes made his heart tense with uncertainty.

"You're allowed to be happy," Cherry reminded him one evening. "Even if it's new. Even if it feels like you have to fight for it."

And so, he fought quietly: by showing up, by laughing, by letting himself feel every layer of warmth Ethan offered, and by learning to navigate the slight unpredictability of Ethan's moods. A smile that flickered, a word left unspoken, a gentle hesitation, Felix recognised them not as failures, but as signs that love could be real, even when complicated.

Lying beside Ethan, watching shadows stretch across the ceiling, Felix realised that love wasn't one perfect moment. It wasn't grand gestures or fairytale clarity. It was messy, tender, and sometimes uncertain. It was the choice to stay, to be present, and to allow someone in, fully, even when they weren't always perfectly predictable.

Messy. Beautiful. Brave.

And maybe, just maybe, it was worth it.

CHAPTER THIRTEEN

Borrowed Time

Felix didn't realise how fast time moved until he watched it in Ethan's rearview mirror.

Every weekend blurred into the next, stolen moments between shifts, tired train rides, hurried text messages. Felix's life had changed pace entirely. The boy who once measured time in homework deadlines and stage rehearsals now counted it in departures and arrivals, in the blink of a phone screen lighting up, in the beat before Ethan's voice said, *"Hey, I'm here."*

He had turned down the creative arts course. No one had expected him to, least of all himself. But something inside had shifted, a quiet rebellion against a life so carefully pre-planned by others. He wasn't entirely sure who he was yet, or who he wanted to become, but he knew he wanted the space to figure it out without someone else's spotlight burning down on him.

He worked part-time at a local bookshop now, the kind with creaky floorboards, slow mornings, and shelves that always needed restocking. It was humble, small, and safe. And in the stillness of it, Felix found peace, a chance to breathe, to live quietly for a while, without the weight of expectation pressing him down.

Ethan remained a constant. Their connection had deepened quickly, yet he still carried a flicker of mystery. Ethan's warmth was there, always, but so were the pauses, little silences that stretched just long enough to make Felix notice. A delayed reply. A glance that seemed distant. A teasing word with an edge Felix couldn't quite read. It wasn't cruel. It wasn't intentional. But it was enough to make Felix's chest tighten, to remind him that even the happiest moments were never fully guaranteed.

Cherry had noticed it too.

"Do you feel like you know all of him?" she asked one evening as they walked along the Thames, the city's lights reflecting like scattered sequins in the water.

Felix hesitated. "Most of him," he said. "Enough of him."

Cherry's gaze softened, protective. "Just promise me if something doesn't feel right, you won't pretend it does."

He nodded, but the words clung to him, sticking like dust on damp skin.

Still, he clung to the good. And there was so much good. Days spent exploring hidden corners of London, stumbling across tiny cafés, or slipping into obscure museums no one else seemed to visit. Long drives with music blasting, singing off-key, laughter spilling out into the night. One night, they danced in the headlights of Ethan's car on an empty country road, arms flailing, breathless from joy and late-night air. It was chaos. It was magic.

Yet even in those perfect moments, Felix felt the faint tug of caution. Ethan's warmth was real, but so were the subtle signals that made Felix question: was he fully there, or was part of him always holding back? The thought unsettled him, but instead of retreating, he tried to meet it with patience, a quiet reminder that love could be messy, beautiful, and brave all at once.

His room remained sacred. Everything in its place, Amber CDs stacked, posters pinned perfectly, wax melts perfuming the air with faint vanilla and lavender. Cherry still dropped by often, perched on the edge of his bed while Felix pressed play on the latest Amber video, narrating every move, outfit, and lyric with reverent enthusiasm.

"You're obsessed," she teased.

"She's iconic," Felix replied without missing a beat.

Ethan sometimes watched too, sitting quietly, arms folded, teasing only when Felix insisted on watching the same video three times in a row. And yet, even in those small rituals, Felix could feel the ebb and flow of their connection. Ethan's presence was steady, yes, but occasionally unpredictable, a lingering glance, a word half-spoken, a sudden quiet that made Felix ache just a little.

As Felix closed his eyes one night, he couldn't ignore the small knot in his chest, a whisper of something approaching, something that would test the fragile rhythm he'd worked so hard to build.

Ethan was there, present and warm, yet sometimes just out of reach. Little pauses, fleeting silences, things left unsaid, threads that made Felix wonder how much he truly understood, and how much remained just out of view.

He let himself breathe anyway, letting the good moments wash over him. The laughter, the music, the stolen drives, the quiet evenings, it was all real. And yet, as he lay awake later that night, Felix couldn't ignore the tiny whisper at the edge of his thoughts: *What if the spaces between us aren't so small after all?*

Even as he closed his eyes again, he knew that the next chapter of this story, of him, of Ethan, of what it meant to risk love, was waiting to unfold.

CHAPTER FOURTEEN

The Space Between

Felix began to notice it in the silences, the small knots, the tiny spaces that had been whispering at the edge of his chest for weeks.

Not the comfortable ones, the kind he and Cherry fell into while people-watching from a bench or sipping coffee on opposite sides of a quiet table. No, these were different. These silences arrived mid-conversation with Ethan, heavy and uncertain, like a pause that didn't quite know what it was waiting for.

It wasn't anything dramatic. There was no fallout, no confrontation, no reason to panic. Just… a growing space between them. And space had always made Felix uneasy.

He tried to fill it at first, with inside jokes, long messages, plans for the weekend. He offered more than he had, stretching himself like clingfilm over something that felt increasingly fragile.

Ethan responded, of course. Still came by, still smiled that same smile, still made Felix feel like the centre of the universe when he was near. But something had shifted. His answers were shorter. His stories less vivid. There were moments when he was there, physically, but not quite with him.

Cherry saw it before Felix was ready to admit it.

They were walking home together one evening, Felix's tote bag filled with secondhand storybooks and the faint scent of roasted coffee beans trailing behind them. The city buzzed around them, sirens, laughter, mopeds screeching through narrow gaps, but between them, there was a kind of quiet that asked for truth.

Cherry glanced over at him, her expression softening as a thought flickered behind her eyes, a memory.

She'd met Ethan once before, briefly, on one of those rare afternoons when Felix had managed to get both worlds to overlap. He'd invited

Cherry over after work, promising pizza and music (Amber, of course), and Ethan had shown up halfway through, hair still damp from a shower, leaning in the doorway with that easy grin of his. The three of them had sat in Felix's room, surrounded by the soft hum of an old Now… That's What I Call Music CD playing in the background, fairy lights catching on Ethan's watch every time he moved his hand.

Felix had been alive in a way Cherry hadn't seen before, animated, glowing, his voice tumbling over itself with excitement as he shared stories and made Ethan laugh. She'd watched him gesture wildly, grinning when Ethan interrupted with something teasing, and Cherry had felt this quiet warmth seeing her best friend so certain, so safe in that moment.

Still, even then, something subtle had stirred beneath the surface. There were fleeting seconds, tiny pauses between sentences, where Ethan's gaze seemed to wander, soft but unreadable. Cherry had noticed it without meaning to. A kind of distance behind his smile, like he was both present and already halfway gone.

Now, as Felix walked beside her through the cool night air, that memory returned uninvited, the same boy she'd seen once looking at Felix like he held the whole world, and the quiet ache of knowing that look had changed.

"He doesn't look at you the way he used to," Cherry said softly.

Felix blinked. "He's just tired lately."

Cherry didn't push. She never did. But her silence carried weight, a kind of stillness that Felix had come to recognise as love, even when it was hard to receive.

Later that night, Ethan cancelled again. Last-minute. No real reason. Felix stared at the message for a long time, thumb hovering above the keyboard, before simply replying: *Okay, maybe next week x.*

He didn't cry. Not this time. He just lay back in bed, Amber's voice playing quietly through his speakers, the shadows from his fairy lights flickering across the wall like ghosts that couldn't sit still.

And then, as if on cue, Cherry called.

"Get dressed. I'm outside."

He didn't ask questions. He just grabbed his hoodie and slipped into his trainers.

They drove in silence at first, Cherry's hand occasionally tapping the steering wheel in time with the music. *'Oliver Twist'* - the song of 2011, and the soundtrack to many Cherry and Felix late night drives. After twenty minutes, they reached a viewpoint overlooking the city. The skyline shimmered beneath them, full of stories that didn't belong to them but somehow made them feel less alone.

Felix exhaled. "What if I'm too much?"

Cherry turned toward him sharply. "You're not."

"But what if—"

"No," she said, more firmly now. "Felix, if someone makes you feel like your love is too loud, it's because they're not ready to hear it."

He looked away. "It's not even that he's done anything. It's more the way it feels. Like something's slipping through my hands, and I don't know how to stop it."

"Then let it slip," Cherry said gently. "If someone wants to stay, they will. And if they don't, you don't need to keep the door open for someone who's already halfway out."

The words sat between them, raw and kind at the same time.

Felix nodded, but he didn't say anything. Instead, he leaned his head against the window and watched the city sparkle.

They stayed like that for over an hour. No rush. No need to pretend.

Over the next week, things with Ethan didn't fall apart. But they didn't fall together either. There were more missed calls. A few odd moments where Ethan laughed at the wrong time, or forgot things Felix had already told him. And then there were the pictures, small tags from mutual friends, nights out Ethan hadn't mentioned, flashes of him in places he claimed not to be going.

Nothing major. Nothing concrete. Just… threads.

Felix didn't accuse. He wasn't sure what he'd even say. Instead, he journaled more. He stayed late at the bookshop and rearranged entire shelves just for the peace it brought him. He spent more time with Cherry, who made no comment when he showed up at her door with a takeaway and tired eyes.

One night, the three of them had planned to go out, Ethan, Cherry, and Felix. It would have been the first time Cherry and Ethan *properly* met. Felix had imagined it a dozen different ways, obsessing over the dynamics, what they'd think of each other, if Ethan would even show up on time.

But fifteen minutes before they were meant to meet, his phone lit up.

Something came up. I'm so sorry. Next time, promise. x

Felix didn't reply.

Cherry arrived anyway, and they walked along the South Bank with paper cups of hot chocolate, their laughter gradually pushing the disappointment into the background.

"I think I need to press pause," Felix said, finally.

Cherry just squeezed his hand.

CHAPTER FIFTEEN

Fractured Reflections

The weight of quiet doubts settled on Felix's chest like the thick fog that often rolled in from the river, slow and subtle at first, curling through every corner of his mind, until it became all-consuming, pressing him down until breathing felt heavy.

Each unanswered message from Ethan chipped away at the mirror Felix held up to himself. That mirror, once clear and bright with hope, now showed fractures that twisted his reflection into something unfamiliar. The boy who had smiled so easily, who dreamed so openly, was still there beneath the cracks, but harder to recognise. Every pause in Ethan's replies stretched longer than the last, and the warmth they once shared flickered like a candle struggling against a cold draft.

Felix told himself love wasn't supposed to be perfect, that there were ups and downs in every relationship, but something gnawed deeper in his gut, a whisper of unease he couldn't shake.

He tried not to let it grow. Tried to convince himself that distance didn't mean disinterest, that people got busy, that everyone carried shadows they wouldn't always reveal. But secrets, Felix knew, had a way of demanding to be seen, like a shadow shifting in the corner of your eye, impossible to ignore no matter how hard you looked away.

That evening, after nearly two days of silence from Ethan, Felix sat alone in his room. The soft glow of Amber's posters bathed the walls in a golden hue, the familiar images a quiet comfort amid the storm in his chest. He traced his fingers over the smooth surface of a CD case, then picked up his phone, scrolling through old conversations, hoping, searching, desperate for some clue or sign, some thread to pull him from the twisting ache inside.

The sudden buzz of his phone startled him, breaking the silence like a lifeline.

It was a message from Cherry.

"Can we talk? I'm worried about you."

His fingers trembled as he stared at the words, unsure if he was ready to face what that conversation might hold. After a moment, he typed back simply, *"Yeah, sure, when?"*

The next day, they met at their favourite café, a small place tucked between two busy streets, with chipped tiles and the kind of espresso that tasted like burnt caramel and possibility. Cherry's eyes were serious, steady, as she slid a steaming cup across the table toward him.

"Felix," she said softly, "you don't have to carry everything alone. You know that, right?"

He swallowed the lump in his throat, nodding. Words caught in the tight knot of his chest.

"I just hate seeing you like this," she continued, voice gentle but unwavering. "You've always been the one to bring light, to STAY HAPPY no matter what. But it's okay to admit when things aren't okay. Especially with Ethan."

The sting of her words hit harder than he expected. The truth was raw and fragile. He'd been holding on to a fragile hope, a hope that Ethan was still the person he believed him to be. That maybe the silences were just pauses, not endings.

Cherry's concern felt like a lifeline, pulling him back from the edge of denial, forcing him to confront the fracture spreading quietly through his heart.

That night, Felix lay awake in his perfectly arranged room, the city hum outside his window a distant murmur. Amber's posters glowed faintly on the walls, candles flickering shadows that danced in the corners. He stared at the ceiling, thoughts swirling like the mist outside, knowing, deep down, something had to change. He needed to reclaim himself, not just for the sake of love, but for the boy who once dreamed of bright stages and endless possibilities.

Maybe, just maybe, the answer wouldn't come from Ethan. Maybe it would come from somewhere else entirely. Somewhere unexpected.

CHAPTER SIXTEEN

The Road That Vanished

The night didn't feel dangerous.

It felt numb.

Felix walked the long way home with Amber's voice in his ears, the only thing lately that made him feel tethered to the world. His breath fogged in the cold air, the sky a smudged charcoal above him. He kept his hood up, shoulders tight, fingers balled in his pockets like he was holding himself together from the inside.

It hadn't happened all at once, the heaviness, the quiet collapse. It had built over years, layered like sediment.

The childhood he never talked about.
The teacher whose hands had rewritten the way Felix understood safety.
The silence that followed him into adulthood like a shadow.

People assumed PTSD came from a single moment, a shock, a catastrophe. They didn't understand that sometimes it came from being hurt before you ever knew how to defend yourself… and then being hurt again and again in different, quieter ways.

Tonight, it all felt too loud inside him.

Geo's betrayal lingered like a bruise, the friend who pretended to care, who wanted control more than connection. The boy Felix once thought might be safe had turned out to be just another lesson in letting go of people who wear masks.

Then Ethan, sweet, complicated Ethan, who made Felix feel alive one minute and invisible the next. Mixed signals. Missed calls. Promises that evaporated. The sting of hope turning sour. Felix had spent months trying to decipher what he meant to Ethan, until the questions themselves hollowed him out.

Bullying, too, years of it. First for being "too soft," then for his weight, which swung like a pendulum depending on whether he was coping or barely coping. People laughed. Whispered. Moved on with their lives. They never realised their words stayed in him long after they forgot they'd said them.

Everyone moved on.

Felix carried everything.

Tonight, he was tired of carrying.

He looked both ways out of habit… but his mind wasn't on the road.

It was somewhere far behind him, in childhood rehearsal rooms, in quiet bedrooms, in kitchen cupboards, in whispered arguments with Ethan, in every moment he'd ever been told to be quiet, be small, be grateful.

He stepped out.

Headlights.

A horn.

A screech that ripped the night open.

Then, impact.

The world slammed sideways. Pain shot white through his body. His headphones flew. Amber's voice cut out mid-chorus. The pavement rushed up and swallowed him in a cold he couldn't breathe through.

The car didn't stop.

It didn't even slow.

It vanished into the dark, leaving Felix broken on the road that had been empty seconds before.

His legs felt disconnected. His vision blurred into stardust. He couldn't tell if he was screaming or if the noise was only in his head.

For a moment, a terrifying, peaceful moment…

…he wondered if this was the end.

And if maybe that wasn't the worst thing.

He thought of Ethan.
He thought of Cherry.
He thought of a version of himself he had been trying to outrun since he was ten years old.
And then he thought of his mum.

His chest tightened in a way the impact hadn't caused.

He wasn't ready to leave her alone with that kind of grief.

It was Begonia who saved him.

She felt it before she knew it.

A mother's instinct, sharp, primal. She'd been pacing, checking her phone every few seconds, telling herself not to spiral. But something *pulled* her, like a thread snapping in her chest. She grabbed her keys with shaking hands and left the house without a coat.

She found him by a flickering streetlamp, one trainer half off, blood on the concrete forming rivers the rain tried to erase.

Her scream was the kind that lived in nightmares.

She dropped beside him, brushing hair off his forehead with trembling fingers, whispering his name over and over as if the repetition alone could anchor him to the world.

Her voice cracked.

"Please don't leave me, Felix. Please."

The hospital was an assault of light and sound, bright strips above him, beeping machines that felt louder than breathing. The nurses spoke in rushed fragments. Begonia clutched his hand like she was holding his soul inside his body.

Felix drifted in and out, but the physical pain was nothing compared to the internal collapse.

Because the accident wasn't the cause of his PTSD.

It was the final blow.

The culmination of a lifetime of swallowed trauma.

He lay there staring at the ceiling tiles and realised something devastating:

Every person who ever hurt him got to move on.

The teacher.
The bullies.
Geo.
Ethan, who still texted like nothing was wrong.
All of them went home, laughed, slept peacefully.

And Felix was the one in a hospital bed, stitched together by machines and a mother's prayers.

A cruel part of him wondered if maybe he was never meant to stay. If maybe he wasn't built for a world that seemed to demand strength from wounds he never got to heal.

His eyes slid shut.

The darkness rose like a tide.

And then, through the haze, he heard it.

Amber's voice.

Soft.
Shaky.
Playing from Begonia's phone, held close to his ear like a lifeline.

"I'm stronger than yesterday…"

The song he had clung to through childhood.
Through loneliness.
Through the quiet pain no one ever saw.

Now, it felt like someone was fighting beside him.

Begonia's hand squeezed his.

"Stay with me, sweetheart. I'm right here."

And Felix, for the first time in months, wanted to try.

He didn't die that night.

But a part of him did, the part that believed silence kept him safe, that he was meant to endure instead of heal.

Recovery was slow. The trauma didn't fade; it simply changed shape. Some days he'd wake shaking. Other days he'd dissociate until hours vanished. The doctor said PTSD, but the word felt too small for a lifetime of ghosts.

Still, Felix kept breathing.

Cherry visited often. She didn't ask him to be strong. She didn't tell him to get over it. She just held his hand and said, "You scare me when you disappear. Don't disappear."

He didn't answer. But he heard her.

One night, when the house was quiet and Begonia had fallen asleep in the armchair beside him, Felix reached for his laptop with trembling fingers.

He opened a blank document.

He didn't know what he was writing toward, forgiveness, survival, truth. Maybe all of it.

All he knew was that he couldn't keep swallowing the darkness. He had to turn it into something. Something that might keep someone else alive.

He typed two words.

The same mantra Amber had given him as a child.
The same phrase Begonia whispered when his world collapsed.
The same thing he was determined, somehow, to do.

STAY HAPPY.
And for the first time, he didn't write it as a lie.
He wrote it as a promise.

CHAPTER SEVENTEEN

The First Spark

Healing wasn't linear. Felix learned that the hard way.

Some mornings, he woke up with fire in his chest, determination, purpose, something close to joy. Other mornings, he didn't want to get out of bed at all. The shadows still whispered. The flashbacks still came. A song on the radio, a tyre screech in the distance, the sterile smell of antiseptic, they all tugged him back to that night, uninvited and relentless.

But something *was* different now.

He had survived.

And that survival came with a stubborn defiance, a need to create, to *speak*, to prove that what happened to him hadn't destroyed him. Not completely.

It began quietly.

A single video, filmed from his bed, propped up by a stack of books and trembling hope. His voice was softer than usual, uncertain around the edges. No intro, no editing, just Felix, pale, recovering, eyes tired but awake.

"Hi," he said, blinking into the lens. "This isn't… easy for me to talk about. But I need to do it. For me, and maybe for someone else who needs to hear it."

He spoke for nearly an hour. About the accident. The PTSD. The fear. The guilt of surviving when it would've been easier not to. He didn't mention Ethan. He didn't have to.

At the end, he looked straight at the camera and said:

"I've spent years pretending I was okay. But I wasn't. And I won't do that anymore. This is me. Healing. Slowly. Messily. But still here. Still trying to STAY HAPPY."

He hit upload before he could change his mind.

And that was the beginning.

The messages trickled in first, quiet thanks from strangers who'd never seen someone say the things they'd been too afraid to feel. Then came the follows. The shares. The comment that said, *"You saved my life tonight"*

It overwhelmed Felix. In the best and worst ways.

He wasn't used to being seen, not like this. Not for his vulnerability. But it felt real. More real than any performance he'd ever given on a stage.

Cherry watched him grow into it, not into fame, but into himself.

"You're helping people just by being honest," she said one afternoon, curled beside him on the floor of his room, surrounded by camera gear and scribbled notes.

"I'm just telling my story," Felix replied, fiddling with the lens cap.

"Exactly," she said. "And that's brave."

He smiled, though it still felt strange to think of himself as brave. Survival hadn't felt like courage, it had felt like scraping through by his fingernails.

But maybe courage looked different when you lived with ghosts.

As the weeks turned into months, *STAY HAPPY* became more than a phrase. It was a project. A channel. A quiet revolution.

Felix began documenting the small moments, making wax melts in his kitchen with scents inspired by his childhood, visiting places that once held fear and reclaiming them with laughter, sitting down to talk openly about mental health, healing, and hope.

He didn't pretend to have all the answers.

But he was no longer ashamed of the questions.

Begonia would sometimes watch from the doorway, pretending to tidy or sort laundry, but really just listening. She never interfered, never asked him to tone it down. She simply let him *be,* and that, in its own way, was healing, too.

"I'm proud of you," she told him once, eyes shining. "Not just for what you're doing… but for coming back."

He didn't reply. He just wrapped his arms around her and let her hold him, for the first time in years, without pulling away too soon.

Felix was still fragile.

Still figuring out who he was without the weight of other people's expectations. Still missing Ethan some days more than he wanted to admit. Still recovering.

But something inside him had shifted again.
Not a scream this time.
A spark.
A whisper.
STAY HAPPY. And this time, he meant it.

CHAPTER EIGHTEEN

When the Light Came Back

Felix didn't notice the message at first.

He was too busy. Too caught up in the gentle chaos of everything *STAY HAPPY* had become. What began as a whisper into the dark had grown louder, not just a YouTube channel now, but a small movement.

His wax melts sold out after a creator with thousands of followers mentioned them in a story. Then came emails from people asking if he'd consider a podcast, a pop-up stall, maybe even a live Q&A event.

Felix laughed when Cherry brought it up. "Me? Talk live in front of people?"

"You used to sing solo on stage in front of hundreds," she pointed out. "You can do this."

But it wasn't the same. That was acting, a mask, a performance. *This* was him. Raw, real, scarred. But for once, he was beginning to believe that people *wanted* to see that version of him.

The message was buried under a sea of Instagram DMs, lost in a folder he rarely checked. It was only when he couldn't sleep one night, nerves buzzing before a filmed collab the next day, that he scrolled past it.

Hey Felix. I saw your video. The one about the accident.

His stomach dropped.

I've watched it three times now. I don't know what I expected. But it wasn't that. You've always been honest, but this... this was something else. I miss you. I miss us.

No name.

But he didn't need one.

He read it again. And again. His pulse quickened, not just from emotion, but from confusion, from *everything*. He hadn't heard from Ethan in months. Their last conversation had been strained, awkward, unfinished. Felix had never told him about the accident. Never said goodbye, either.

And now, here he was. A ghost from another life, watching Felix build a new one.

Cherry saw the difference in him straight away.

"You okay?" she asked gently, handing him his coffee before their filming session.

"Ethan messaged me."

Her brow raised. "And… how do you feel about that?"

Felix shook his head. "I don't know. Angry. Relieved. Scared. Stupid."

"You're allowed all of that," she said, touching his arm. "But you need to ask yourself if you're looking back… or forward."

Felix stared into his cup. "Maybe both."

Ethan didn't push. That surprised Felix.

A second message came two days later. Just a YouTube link — *STAY HAPPY, Ep 2: Healing Isn't Linear* - with a single line beneath it:

I never stopped believing in you. I just forgot how to believe in myself.

It took Felix a week to reply.

They met in a park, quiet and tucked away behind a café Felix had loved as a teenager. Ethan stood waiting by the bench, older, a little tired, but exactly the same in the ways that mattered, the soft eyes, the nervous fingers twitching at his sides, the way he smiled like it hurt a little to hope.

"Hey," Felix said, unsure whether to laugh or cry.

"Hey," Ethan replied, stepping closer.

There was a long silence. Then Ethan added, "I'm sorry. For disappearing. For shutting down. I was scared. And selfish. And I didn't know how to be what you needed."

Felix swallowed hard. "You didn't need to be anything except honest."

"I wasn't," Ethan admitted. "But I've changed. And you… you've grown into someone I always knew was there, just waiting to come alive."

They sat. Talked. Cried, a little. And then, eventually, laughed.

It wasn't perfect. But it was *possible*.

The next *STAY HAPPY* video was different.

Felix sat with Ethan beside him this time, their knees touching, a coffee, and mug of tea between them and nerves dancing across their shared smile.

"Today's video is about second chances," Felix said to the camera. "And how sometimes… healing circles back around."

Ethan looked straight into the lens.

"I left when I should've stayed. I was afraid. And I hurt him. But watching him share his story, knowing what he's survived, reminded me that real love doesn't quit. It waits. It learns. It returns."

The response was overwhelming.

Some cheered. Some questioned. Most just *felt* it, the way you feel truth in your bones even if it's not perfect.

Felix and Ethan didn't rush.

They moved slowly. With care. Rebuilding, not rewriting. There were still questions. Still healing. But they were doing it together.

STAY HAPPY continued to grow, not just as a brand, but as a lifeline for people who had been through their own darkness. Felix launched a small online store. Held his first live event. Started a podcast.

He called the first episode: *You're not Alone, Even when it feels like it.*

And by the end of it, he knew this was no longer just his story. It belonged to everyone who had ever clawed their way back from the edge.

But still, at its heart, was that boy from Chapter One.

Scared. Dreaming. Waiting to be loved.

And now, finally, loved right back.

CHAPTER NINETEEN

Becoming Felix Asher

Fame, or whatever Felix was experiencing now, didn't arrive in a rush of paparazzi or flashing cameras.

It came gently. Like a hand on your shoulder in a quiet room.

The first time someone recognised him in public, it was at a train station. Felix had been waiting in line for a coffee, headphones in, scrolling through comments on his latest *STAY HAPPY* video, an episode where he spoke about finding safety in small routines, and the comfort of things that never asked questions.

A girl about his age tapped him lightly on the shoulder.

"Sorry," she said, cheeks pink, "are you Felix Asher?"

He blinked. Took a second. Then nodded.

"I just wanted to say thank you. Your video about PTSD helped me feel seen. I showed it to my mum. We watched it together. We cried with you."

Felix didn't know what to say. He stumbled out a thank you and gave her a hug, shaky and surprised. When she left, coffee in hand, he sat on a bench for ten minutes just to breathe.

That's when it really hit him: people were *listening*.

And not just listening, *hearing* him.

Stay Happy had grown into something neither of them had fully planned for. What began as a few videos, wax melts, and a small message of hope had become its own movement. People wrote in from across the world, some sharing their own stories of survival, others simply saying: "I needed this today."

Felix didn't always feel worthy of it.

Some mornings, he still woke up with the old fear humming beneath his ribs, fear that it could all go away, or that he wasn't doing enough, or that someone would look behind the curtain and see just how messy his healing really was.

But each time the doubts crept in, he reminded himself: *This wasn't about being perfect. It never was.*

He wasn't trying to be a guru, or a brand, or even an influencer. He was just telling his truth, and inviting people to sit in it with him, without shame.

Ethan watched it all unfold with quiet awe. He was supportive, but never pushy. He didn't try to insert himself into Felix's spotlight. He showed up, helped pack wax melt orders, filmed behind-the-scenes clips for Instagram, brought Felix coffee between podcast recordings.

Sometimes they'd sit side by side, reading through messages from viewers.

"Feels unreal, doesn't it?" Ethan would say.

Felix always nodded. "It does. But… it feels *right*, too."

Then came the email.

Subject: Possible Feature – BBC One Documentary Series

Felix read it three times before showing Cherry.

"You *have* to say yes," she said, wide-eyed.

"I don't know…" he replied, heart pounding. "What if I'm not ready?"

"Felix. You've *been* ready. You just didn't know it yet."

It was a chance to tell his story on a bigger platform, from the accident, to the mental health battle, to *STAY HAPPY*. The producers weren't interested in sugar-coating it. They wanted the real thing. Felix's voice, Felix's words. Felix's heart.

He agreed.

Filming started quietly, woven into his day-to-day. The cameras followed him through wax-making sessions, podcast recordings, even a trip back to the street where the hit-and-run happened. Begonia appeared briefly, nervous but proud, her voice cracking as she spoke about the night she found her son lying broken and unconscious on the pavement, and the strength it took to help him come back from that edge.

"I nearly lost him," she said to the camera. "But he didn't let go. He stayed. And now he's teaching other people how to stay too."

The documentary aired on a rainy Sunday night.

By Monday morning, #STAYHAPPY was trending.

Felix's inbox was flooded. Brands reached out. Journalists. Schools asking him to come speak. People sent photos of their 'STAY HAPPY' hoodies hanging in bedrooms, worn at therapy sessions, taken on holiday.

One girl messaged: *"My brother took his own life last year. I was heading in the same direction. Your story pulled me back. Thank you for staying."*

Felix read the message aloud to Ethan, voice trembling.

"I didn't save her," he whispered.

"No," Ethan said, placing a hand on his. "You *reminded* her that she could save herself."

Felix stood by his bedroom window that night, looking out across the city skyline, lights blinking like stars.

The boy he'd once been, afraid, overlooked, unheard, was still with him.

But now, that boy had a voice. A platform. A purpose.

Felix Asher hadn't been born on a stage. He'd been built slowly, through loss and laughter, through trauma and recovery, through the quiet courage of choosing to stay — again and again.

And *STAY HAPPY* wasn't just his brand.

It was his anthem.

A promise he'd made to himself.

And now, a lifeline he was handing to the world.

CHAPTER TWENTY

The Weight of the Light

The noise had changed.

It wasn't the chaos of trauma anymore, not the kind that roared through Felix's body and left him shaking. It was a different noise now: email pings, booking requests, podcast inquiries, wax melt restocks, merchandise launches, and a fanbase that kept growing by the day.

Some days, Felix barely recognised the life he'd built.

He had a team now… Just a small one, Cherry at the helm, still his closest anchor, helping run the *STAY HAPPY* online store, the wax melt collection, the podcast schedule, and an ever-expanding social media following. He'd never set out to be a brand, but somehow, he'd become one.

And yet, when it was quiet, when the ring light clicked off and the front door was locked, Felix still felt most like himself sitting cross-legged on the floor with a coffee in his Amber mug, surrounded by wax samples and hand-labeled packages. There was something sacred about the smallness of it all. The intimacy.

The world wanted more of him now, but he was learning he didn't have to give it all away.

Public life had its price.

There were moments where Felix felt exposed in ways he hadn't anticipated. People commented on everything: his clothes, his voice, how tired he looked. Some assumed they knew him, as though watching his story unfold gave them ownership of it.

One night, after an unusually invasive comment about his body went viral on a gossip thread, Felix locked himself in the bathroom and cried until he couldn't feel his face.

Ethan sat outside the door for over an hour, quietly speaking through it. "You are more than what they see. You're not their mirror, You're your own."

It helped. But it also reminded Felix just how heavy the light could be.

Still, the good outweighed the ache.

He was invited to speak at schools, mental health events, creative festivals. Sometimes, standing on those stages, he'd look out into the sea of faces, young people, quiet, open, hopeful, and feel the words pouring out of him like they'd been waiting there all along.

Not polished. Not perfect.

Just true.

He spoke about survival. About the night of the hit-and-run. About how darkness wasn't always dramatic, sometimes it was just the absence of feeling anything at all. And about how healing wasn't linear. How some mornings, you had to drag yourself out of bed and make yourself believe in the light, even when it felt fake.

"And then one day," he often said at the end of his talks, "the light isn't fake anymore. It's just yours. And it's waiting for you to stop running from it."

He always ended the same way.

Stay happy. Even if it's messy. Especially if it's messy.
Back at home, he and Ethan had carved out something peaceful.

They cooked together, watched old films, took long walks in the rain. Ethan didn't try to fix Felix's bad days. He simply made space for them, warm, open, honest. There was a comfort in that. A steadiness.

They didn't post much online about each other. Their love felt too personal to be content.

But everyone who saw Felix glow in Ethan's presence knew.

He was loved. Properly. Gently.

One afternoon, after recording a new episode of *STAY HAPPY*, Cherry sat across from Felix in the studio. They were surrounded by cushions, mic cords tangled like vines, the scent '*STAY POSITIVE*' still hanging in the air from a nearby wax burner.

Cherry smiled. "Can I ask you something?"

"Always."

"Do you feel like you've healed?"

Felix didn't answer right away.

He looked around, at the posters on the walls, the pile of amber-scented test samples, the neon '*STAY HAPPY*' sign glowing quietly in the corner.

"I feel like I'm becoming," he said.

And that was enough.

CHAPTER TWENTY-ONE

Foundations

Felix no longer woke up with a weight in his chest. There were still days when the memories came uninvited, the dark roads, the silence, the spinning ache of everything he'd survived, but they didn't *own* him anymore.

Instead, his mornings were filled with slow light, the smell of coffee drifting in from the kitchen, and the low hum of Ethan playing music from his phone while frying eggs in a pan too small for his ambition.

Their flat was tiny, cluttered with candles, recording equipment, and enough thrifted artwork to start a gallery, but it felt like *home*. Not just a place to exist, but a place to *belong*. Felix had painted the bedroom walls himself, patchy in places, uneven in others, but Ethan had laughed and called it "perfectly lived in." The imperfection suited them.

STAY HAPPY was growing. Orders came in faster now, sometimes more than they could handle. What had started as a quiet rebellion, a phrase whispered in the dark, was now something tangible, real, and reaching people far beyond what Felix could've imagined.

He spent his mornings hand-pouring wax melts, afternoons packing boxes, evenings filming new episodes for the *STAY HAPPY* YouTube channel. And through it all, Ethan was never far. He helped design labels, snapped behind-the-scenes photos, brainstormed new scents while they lay in bed with their kitten 'Nala' resting comfortably at the end of it.

"You know," Ethan said one night, flicking through Felix's notebook of ideas, "this isn't just a brand anymore. It's a movement."

Felix tilted his head. "You think so?"

"I *know* so. You're helping people heal. You're giving them something to hold onto."

Felix smiled but said nothing. Still, the way Ethan spoke, like he wasn't just an observer but *part* of it, planted something quietly in his mind.

A few days later, Cherry came over with iced lattes and a folder full of social media analytics. She'd unofficially become Felix's brand advisor, tracking growth, watching trends, keeping him grounded. She was sharp-eyed, supportive, and honest, the perfect voice when Felix doubted himself.

"Have you ever thought about bringing someone on officially?" she asked, scrolling through her phone. "Like, a partner? This is bigger than a one-man show now."

Felix shrugged. "I don't know… I like the control. *STAY HAPPY* is my baby"

Cherry smirked. "That's not what you said when Ethan redesigned your candle packaging."

He rolled his eyes but couldn't help the warmth in his chest. Truthfully, he had thought about it, not just handing off tasks, but *sharing* the vision. Not because he needed help, but because he wanted someone beside him. Someone who knew the cracks and the beauty. Someone who had *seen it all.*

The idea lingered.

But for now, Felix stayed focused. He had a video to film, a letter to his younger self. He sat at his desk, the camera blinking red, and began:

"Hey. I know you're scared right now. I know everything feels like it's falling apart, and you're wondering if it's ever going to get better. But it does. It *really* does…"

The words flowed like water. Not perfect, not rehearsed, but true. Behind the lens, Ethan watched, silent but present, the way he always was.

After filming, Felix reached out and took Ethan's hand.

"Thank you," he whispered.

Ethan kissed his knuckles gently. "For what?"

"For never giving up on me. Even when I gave up on myself."

They didn't need more than that. The story was still unfolding, but the foundations were set. Love, healing, purpose.

And the whisper of something even bigger on the horizon.

CHAPTER TWENTY-TWO

Building Something That Lasts

The kitchen counter was covered in labels, wax paper, and half-folded boxes. A candle flickered gently near the sink, casting golden light across the small space. The chaos had become routine, a comforting kind of mess that marked a life being fully lived.

Felix sat cross-legged on the floor, sorting through orders with a marker in one hand and his phone clutched in the other. Ethan was somewhere behind him, humming under his breath while rinsing mugs, sleeves rolled to the elbow.

They were weeks away from launching the next phase of *STAY HAPPY*: a home scents collection inspired entirely by memory.

Each scent had been carefully crafted, not just for customers, but for *himself*. There was **Playground Rain**, with the sharpness of spring grass and damp concrete that reminded him of school days and skinned knees. **Cinnamon Lamplight**, which captured the feeling of winter in his childhood home, lit with candles and echoing with Begonia's quiet singing. And the one that meant the most, **Road to Healing**, infused with the scent that was a reminder of the calmness after rain, eucalyptus, and something softer… like hope.

Ethan held up a tin in one hand. "This one smells like you."

Felix glanced up. "Is that a compliment?"

Ethan smirked. "It's the best thing I've ever said."

They laughed, a sound that had come back easier in recent months. Not forced. Not masking. Just real.

Felix leaned against the cupboard. "Can I tell you something?"

Ethan looked at him, eyes soft. "Always."

"I never thought I'd be this person," Felix said quietly. "I thought I'd always be… surviving. Floating. Hoping things wouldn't fall apart."

Ethan didn't interrupt.

"But now I'm—" He paused, searching. "I'm *doing* something. With my life. With my pain. And it's because of *you*, Cherry, my mum… and all of this."

He motioned to the boxes, the candles, the tiny business that was no longer so tiny.

Ethan came over and sat beside him, resting his forehead against Felix's.

"You built this," he said. "Not just the brand. Your *life*. You clawed your way back from the edge. I just happened to love you while you did it."

That night, as they packed the final order, Felix tucked a hand-written note into one of the parcels:

"STAY HAPPY - not because life is perfect, but because you're choosing not to let it break you."

The next day, Felix and Cherry met at the café where it all began, the one with the chipped tiles and the espresso that never disappointed. She slid her laptop across the table.

"You ready for this?"

On the screen was a draft: *STAY HAPPY Ltd.* - a registered company. A real one. A full step into the unknown.

Felix stared at it, heart pounding.

He hadn't expected to feel this proud. Or this scared. But he nodded.

"I'm ready."

Cherry smiled. "You'll need a co-director soon. Someone who gets the vision. Someone who can help you grow it."

Felix's thoughts flicked to Ethan.

He didn't say anything then. But he would. When the time was right.

Back home that evening, he lit one of the new candles, the **Road to Healing** one. It filled the room slowly, like a memory making its way back to the surface.

He thought of the boy he used to be.

And then he thought of the man he was becoming.

CHAPTER TWENTY-THREE

Full Circle

The letter arrived on a Tuesday.

A plain white envelope, no return address, just his name written in shaky cursive. Felix turned it over in his hands, hesitant, heart thudding harder than it should for such an ordinary thing.

He didn't open it right away.

Instead, he placed it on the windowsill of his bedroom, the same room that had once felt like a cage and now served as the heart of his healing. The shelves still held every Amber CD, and the scent of eucalyptus wax drifted gently through the air, wrapping around him like a hug from an old friend.

That night, he and Ethan curled into each other on the sofa, their legs tangled under a soft grey blanket. They watched Harry Potter with the volume low, the kind of movie that didn't ask for attention but made you feel something all the same.

Felix didn't mention the letter. Not yet.

The next morning, Cherry popped by with pastries and a bottle of homemade pink lemonade. She'd started calling herself "Chief Brand Fairy," a title Felix never argued with.

They sat at the kitchen table, going over ideas for the upcoming *STAY HAPPY* pop-up event in London, something Cherry had pitched as a "celebration of healing, nostalgia, and community." Felix was nervous about it, but she reminded him that *STAY HAPPY* was no longer just a phrase or even a brand. It was a *movement*.

"You've turned your pain into purpose," she said, her voice softer now. "That takes guts, Felix."

He blinked at her, emotions prickling just behind his eyes. "Do you ever think it's all too much too fast?"

"Sometimes," she said, shrugging. "But you're not alone anymore."

That night, Felix finally opened the letter.

The handwriting belonged to the teacher from stage school. The one he'd tried to forget. The one who had stolen something from him with a hand on his shoulder and a whisper in the dark.

The letter didn't contain an apology, not a real one. Just a hollow reflection, veiled in excuses and insincere regret. Reading it made Felix's skin crawl.

He tore it in half, then again, and again, until it was nothing but confetti at his feet.

But he didn't cry.

Instead, he walked to the bookshelf, pulled out the journal he kept hidden behind his favourite Amber box set, and wrote down three words:

"I forgive myself."

He didn't forgive the man. He never would. But he forgave *himself* for the years of silence, the confusion, the shame that never belonged to him. And that, that felt like freedom.

The following weekend, Felix and Ethan stood together at the pop-up event.

People milled around the bright little venue, breathing in the calming scents, trying on *STAY HAPPY* hoodies, smiling at the handwritten notes slipped into each display.

Ethan leaned in. "You know this is only the beginning, right?"

Felix nodded. "I hope so."

Then, in a moment that felt like a homecoming, Ethan pulled a ring box from his jacket pocket.

It wasn't a proposal. Not yet. Just a simple silver band, a symbol, a promise.

"For the brand," Ethan said. "For the future. For us."

Felix's breath caught. "You want in?"

"I've always been in," Ethan replied. "But now I want to build it *with* you. As your partner, in life, and in business."

Felix smiled, a smile that reached deep into his bones.

The past had left its marks. It always would. But now, it was part of the story, not the end of it.

CHAPTER TWENTY-FOUR

The Stage is Yours

The lights weren't harsh this time.

They didn't blaze down like spotlights trying to burn away every flaw or blind him into silence. Instead, they wrapped around the room like warm sunlight breaking through after a long, cold winter.

Felix stood at the centre of the stage, the microphone cool and familiar in his hand. His palms were damp, a quiet reminder that nerves never truly vanished, but his grip was steady. The *STAY HAPPY Live Experience* had sold out in less than a day, filling this small, intimate theatre in the heart of London with a tapestry of faces: some old friends, some strangers who'd found him through the videos and messages, and some quiet souls who had reached out in whispers, saying things like *you helped me*, *you reminded me I matter*, and *I didn't feel so alone anymore.*

His eyes scanned the crowd and landed first on Cherry, sitting front row, her grin radiant but her eyes shimmering with tears. She caught his gaze and gave him a little nod, their silent way of saying, *we're in this together.*

Beside her sat Ethan, wearing his own *STAY HAPPY* hoodie like a second skin. His presence was a quiet anchor, proud, grounded, present. Watching Felix, he was no longer just the boy Felix once longed for; he was now his partner in everything that *STAY HAPPY* had become.

Behind them were faces Felix recognised from his journey: loyal followers who had stood with him from his very first upload, those who'd watched his world stop with the raw video about the accident, the moment that had shattered him but also set him on this path.

Tonight wasn't about merch sales or follower counts. It wasn't about algorithms or trends.

Tonight was about truth.

Felix drew in a slow breath and began, his voice calm but layered with years of pain and hope.

"I used to think the worst day of my life was the day I was hit by a car, the day I was left broken, bleeding, and forgotten."

A hush rippled through the room, the kind of quiet that holds a collective breath, waiting for what comes next.

"But the worst day," he continued, voice steady now, "was the day after. When I woke up in a hospital bed, surrounded by the sterile hum of machines and strangers' worried faces, and realised… I had to keep going. But I didn't know how."

He paused, letting the weight of that moment settle among them.

"I carried pain that wasn't mine to carry, guilt that tried to crush me under its weight. I blamed myself for being broken. For needing help. For surviving."

His eyes swept across the audience, finding connection in the sea of faces.

"But here's what I've learned: surviving isn't just about making it through the day. It's a victory. Healing isn't a neat, straight path, it's messy, winding, and sometimes you fall back before you move forward. And being sensitive, emotional, hopeful, those things? They're not weaknesses. They're superpowers."

A ripple of applause started, gentle but certain, growing like the first light of dawn.

Felix smiled, warmth spreading through his chest.

"I started *STAY HAPPY* not because I was happy all the time, but because I needed something to believe in on the days I wasn't.

Something real, something honest. Something that could carry me through the dark."

The applause swelled, not loud and flashy but deep and resonant, a shared understanding, a collective *me too*.

Felix stepped back as the stage lights softened and a screen flickered to life behind him.

A short film began to play, a montage of moments stitched together like pieces of a puzzle: the wide-eyed boy from childhood, the shaky first YouTube videos, late-night laughter with Cherry, quiet healing walks with Ethan, the painstaking hours hand-pouring wax melts, tearful confessions on camera, and moments of joy found even in the dark.

And then the final scene, Felix standing alone on a bridge at dawn, the sky slowly brightening behind him as he whispered,

"It's okay to not be okay, just don't give up before your light arrives."

The screen faded to black.

The audience rose to their feet, the applause swelling into a roar of support and love.

Felix didn't cry. Not tonight.

He took a slow, deliberate bow, not as a performer playing a role, but as a survivor.

As a storyteller.

As the boy who had once been lost, but now was leading others home.

CHAPTER TWENTY-FIVE

The journey continues

The applause had finally faded, leaving behind a quiet hum that still vibrated in Felix's chest. It was not the hollow silence of an ending but the steady drumbeat of something new, a beginning, raw and full of possibility.

Backstage, the soft glow of the dressing room lights wrapped around him like a warm embrace. The familiar faces that had been with him through every twist and turn of this journey smiled in quiet celebration. Ethan stood close, offering that same steady, unspoken reassurance, the one that said *we're still here. Together.* Cherry hovered nearby, her eyes bright with pride and a touch of tears, the ever-constant friend who had believed in him long before the world did.

Felix leaned back in his chair, letting the moment wash over him. His mind wandered back to the fractured boy he had once been, the one haunted by silence, drowning in shadows after the accident. The nights he spent grappling with thoughts too heavy to voice, the pain he thought would swallow him whole. All of it wasn't a story he needed to hide anymore. It was a part of him, woven into the very fabric of who he was. Not as scars that weakened him, but as threads that strengthened his soul, giving him the power to rise again.

He thought about the *STAY HAPPY* brand, how it had blossomed far beyond anything he'd dared to dream. What started as a quiet promise to himself, a lifeline thrown out on the darkest days, had grown into a community, a movement. Each video he uploaded, every wax-melt poured by hand, every heartfelt message he shared, was a voice reaching out to those who felt unseen, unheard, and alone. Together, they formed a tapestry of hope, imperfect, messy, but beautifully real.

And then there was Ethan.

Their relationship had deepened in ways Felix hadn't imagined possible. Ethan was no longer just the quiet figure at the edge of the frame but a partner in life and in the heart of *STAY HAPPY*.

His creativity and unwavering belief had shaped the brand's evolution, transforming it into something bigger than a single person's dream. It was theirs, a shared vision built on love, trust, and the courage to keep going.

Felix smiled softly, feeling the weight of the moment settle over him like a gentle promise. There would still be struggles ahead. Healing was never a straight path, and some days would be harder than others. But now, he carried within him a new kind of strength, one born from surviving the storm, from the power of truth, and from the circle of love and support that surrounded him.

He stood, moving to the window where the city lights twinkled in the distance. The night was quiet, but the world was full of noise, stories waiting to be told, lives ready to be touched by the message he carried.

He took a deep breath, the cool air filling his lungs, and whispered the words that had carried him through the darkest nights:

STAY HAPPY. STAY POSITIVE.

Because those words were more than just a slogan. They were a lifeline, a beacon for anyone still searching for their own light.

The journey was far from over.

In fact, it was only just beginning.

Felix turned from the window, his heart steady, his spirit unbroken. Tomorrow, there would be new challenges to face, new stories to share, new people to inspire. But for now, he allowed himself this moment of peace, a quiet celebration of how far he'd come, and the endless possibilities still waiting ahead.

Because *STAY HAPPY* was no longer just his story.

It was theirs.

A promise, a movement, a light in the dark.

And Felix was ready to lead the way.

EPILOGUE

For Anyone Who's Still Searching

If you've made it here, to the final page, to the last word, thank you.

Thank you for walking with me through the memories I once tried to outrun. For holding space for the broken moments and the beautiful ones. For believing that even the most fractured stories can still lead somewhere bright.

There was a time I didn't think I'd make it this far. A time when the silence after the accident felt heavier than the impact itself. When I thought being sensitive made me weak. When I believed that if I showed the world my truth, the anxiety, the trauma, the loneliness, they'd turn away.

But I was wrong.

Because the truth didn't push people away.

It brought them closer.

It brought *you* here.

STAY HAPPY was never about pretending to be okay. It was about learning to hold space for joy even when it hurt. It was about choosing light even when darkness begged you to lie down. It was about remembering that even when life strips everything away... you still have your voice.

And you still matter.

If you're reading this and you're in pain, or lost, or wondering if your story is worth telling, please know this:

You are not alone.

You are not broken.

And there is nothing more powerful than a heart that keeps beating after it's been shattered.

This isn't the end of my story, or yours.

Because the truth is, we are always beginning again.

So wherever you are in your journey...
Take a breath.
Take a step.
Take your time.

And above all else, *STAY HAPPY.*

With love,
Felix Asher

Author's Note

Writing this book wasn't easy.

It meant returning to rooms I'd shut the door on. Revisiting versions of myself I'd tried to outgrow, ignore, or forget. It meant honesty, the kind that shakes you from the inside out.

But it also meant healing.

It meant giving voice to the parts of my story I'd once buried in silence. It meant recognising that the darkness didn't win, because I'm still here. Still trying. Still choosing light every single day.

I chose to tell my truth through fiction, through the eyes of Felix Asher, because sometimes the most honest stories need a little distance to be told safely. Felix gave me the freedom to speak the unspeakable. He allowed me to shape my memories into something creative, something brave, and something that others could see themselves in without feeling alone. Felix is me, and he's also every person who's ever felt broken and still chose to show up.

If this story reached you, comforted you, challenged you, or reminded you that you're not alone, then every page was worth it.

"STAY HAPPY" was never about pretending. It was always about hoping. About holding on through the rough days, and dancing through the good ones. About making space for all the feelings, the joy, the grief, the confusion, the hope.

Thank you for walking this road with me.

The journey continues, but now, we walk it together.

STAY HAPPY
Jack Forrest-Rickard

Thank You

To everyone who stood by me when I had nothing left to give, thank you.

To those who reminded me who I was when I forgot, thank you.

To the strangers who became supporters, and the supporters who became family, thank you.

To the doubters, thank you, too. You taught me how strong I could be.

To every person who reads this and sees themselves in these pages, I wrote this for you. You're not alone. You never were.

And to the boy I used to be.
You made it.
I'm so proud of you.

Printed in Dunstable, United Kingdom